THE TAHOSA MONK

MICHAEL ANTHONY MAY

Auctorem House
276 5th Ave, Ste 704-2591
New York, NY 10001
www.auctoremhouse.com
1.888.332.7718

Dedicated to Reverend Dennis E. Dwyer,
the man who showed me why I'm on this earth:
To entertain....
"United we stand, divided we fall! Give 'em hell!"

—Fr. D. D.

R.I.P.

*Photo courtesy of Maryanne Davis.

Evil and destruction cannot and do not discriminate.
*Evil will always attack first. **It** will always choose its prey.*
***It** chooses the good....*
and kills.

CHARACTERS

The Monk

Ely Whitaker—Justice of the Peace, Mayor and Trading Post owner

George McQuirving—Silver miner

Jakob Mueller—Owner of the Mueller Silver Mine

Johann Mueller—Eldest son of Jakob Mueller

Mrs. Mueller—Wife of Johann Mueller

Erick Mueller—son of Jakob Mueller

Father Paul Kettling—Pastor of Holy Trinity Catholic Church

Ed and Amy Peckman—owners of Peckman's Coffee Shop and Restaurant

Harley McGuire—saloon piano player

Stewart Marcks—owner of Marcks' Saloon

Kevin Marcks—Stewart Marcks' son and saloon employee

Millie Orman—Town seamstress, George's love interest

Asa Helms—farmer and rancher

Eva Helms—fifteen year old daughter of Asa Helms

Josh Adams—silver miner and the town rascal

Del Stigg—town doctor

Monsignor Clemente—investigator from Denver Archdiocese

Father Dennis—investigator from Denver Archdiocese

Fr. Kyle Richardson—Vatican investigator/attorney

Sister Marlena Carmen—Vatican investigator

Monsignor August O'Rourke—Vatican investigator
Fr. Alessio Fabiano—Vatican investigator
Felix—George's mule

PART I

ONE

SATURDAY, SEPTEMBER 6, 1882.

THE MOUNTAINS OF COLORADO.

SILVER MINER GEORGE McQuirving was the first to encounter the strange visitor a few miles from the settlement. The clouds were gray and gloomy and the hard rain pelted his hat. His head was wet but his thick, wool frock coat kept him warm and dry enough for he and his mule, Felix to walk comfortably back to town before nightfall. There was only one narrow trail that led to and from the new Mueller Silver Mine. George traveled it daily along with a number of others and was the last to leave the Mueller today. Tomorrow was Sunday and tonight he wanted to get cleaned up enough for a few drinks and a dance or two with Millie Orman, a new seamstress in town. He'd seen her for the first time just weeks ago. He wasn't entirely convinced that she'd seen him yet, however. Nonetheless, he made up his mind to pursue her and thought of her as he walked.

Through the thick trees as the sun began to set, George could see the faint lights from town. His boots sloshed in the mud puddles. He stumbled once, slipping on the slick slope of the trail, regained his footing and continued when a bright, quick flash of light caught the corner of his eye—pale, almost violet. *Lightning?* he thought. George looked up at the sky and waited for thunder which never came. He trudged onward.

He first heard the huff of what he thought was a horse far away, then the slight rattling of chains against hollow wood. The sounds were coming from a considerable distance behind him. He was sure he'd been the last one out. He shrugged and turned his thoughts back to Millie and the whiskey that was waiting for him.

The rain began to let up a little and he heard the sound again, closer. George turned around and looked to the direction of the mine. He could see it coming down the narrow trail about fifty yards up. The horse he'd heard before wasn't a horse at all, but two oxen. They were huge! Behind them loomed the silhouette of an enormous covered wagon. "What the hell?" he asked aloud. It was the biggest rig he'd ever seen! It was far too big to be coming down that narrow trail. Rocks and branches broke under its weight.

He figured he and Felix ought to get out of the way and squeezed into the dense tree line along the side of the trail.

The huge rig rolled to within a few feet from them. He looked up to the driver's seat and saw the driver wearing what looked like a monk's robe and hood. He couldn't see the man's face. "Evenin'!" he said, backing into the trees further. The driver glanced his way then back to the trail with no reply. The rig came inches from him as it passed. The color of the paint, almost black to him before, now looked more like a dark purple or blue. George felt himself shiver as the wagon slowly creaked by.

Who the hell is this? How did he get that monstrosity up that steep grade? For the first time, George's thoughts didn't go back to the coming night's festivities. Now he felt cold fear but wasn't sure why, exactly. Strange folks were always passing through town, often stopping to sell cheap junk and whatnot, but that was the mine up there, nothing else... nothing else that he knew of anyway.

The wagon continued ahead and George did not feel the need to investigate. He wanted that thing away from him. *Something wrong with that driver*, he thought. George let a distance between them grow and continued toward town.

TWO

TAHOSA, COLORADO 1882. It was nothing more than a mission and trading post with a handful of buildings and a lot more tents and tepees. There was the trading post itself, owned and operated by Ely Whitaker who also served as mayor, sheriff and justice of the peace. Ely was a short, tough, yet stately gentleman who, even in his mid-fifties could still attract the glances of young ladies in town. Much of his business was selling supplies to the local silver miners. His establishment offered lanterns, picks, shovels, axes, flour, apple cider, water jugs and canteens, beans, candles, fresh milk from time to time, baked goods, groceries, hats and guns, oats, chicken feed, just about anything.

There was just one church, Holy Trinity Catholic, whose pastor, Father Paul Kettling ran his mission. He made sure the heavy drinkers and the poorest in the settlement would have a place at night and coffee in the morning. If whites didn't want to bunk with Indians or vice versa in the small church, that was too damned bad. They could play nice or leave, period. The middle aged, grumpy priest was no one to reckon with. Most of the town wasn't even Catholic, but nobody seemed to care. They needed the church and that was that.

There was no bank so everybody packed iron, needless to say.

The small coffee shop and restaurant was run by Ed Peckman and his wife, Amy. In the same building, the settlement's only doctor, Del Stigg lived and held his practice. He stayed relatively busy thanks mostly to miners who'd manage to always injure themselves one way or another.

There were silver miners everywhere. Many of them shared the tent suburbs of the little town about seventy five yards to the west along the banks of the river. Some tents hosted gambling. Others served as bunk houses, a brothel and even small markets and butcher shops.

On the other side of the river lived about eighty members of a Ute Indian tribe. A small log bridge connected the banks.

No one had any way of knowing that within months, the town would be completely abandoned with most of its residents missing, dead or gone. None who would live through the ordeal would be intent on returning.

The small mountain settlement bustled noisily with carriages and wagons, kids playing, miners stocking upcoming and going. Boots thumped on porch boards as folks went about their days.

Most of the residents of Tahosa knew each other and many socialized in the only saloon at night, men and women alike which was generally unheard of anywhere.

Harley McGuire played piano in the saloon every evening except Sundays (with frequent breaks). He wasn't the best player, but he made his living and people liked him. He lived in the back room with the kegs and bottles. Part of his job during the day was to help maintain the place for Stewart Marcks, the owner. Stewart's son Kevin worked as the daytime bartender and sometimes strummed his banjo along with Harley.

Usually, by the afternoons, Harley and Kevin were so smashed it was remarkable Harley could even stay seated on his bench, let alone play. Nonetheless, the place was profitable and functioned accordingly.

It was rumored that the famous Doc Holliday had come through Tahosa earlier that spring and stopped in the saloon. Nobody seemed to really know for sure whether he did or not, however considering the source of the tale. Kevin and Harley's memories of the encounter rapidly became extremely colorful by the time the story was told.

Fact of the matter is, Doctor Henry Holliday *did* pass through town long enough to get off of his mule, buy a bottle of bug juice and take a piss. He was in and gone in five minutes. Of course, according to Harley and Kevin, the three men had become the best of friends by the time he left.

The winters could be bitterly cold with deep snows. Nobody traveled around these mountains during winter unless they absolutely had to.

Crops had come in nicely that season and people were gradually starting to get ready for the coming holidays. The mountains were becoming cooler and the breeze whistled through the thick pines above the valley.

Spawning season for salmon was bountiful. Many folks were busy catching, cleaning and preparing the fish for storage. Hunters left early in the mornings and came back with plenty of venison, rabbit, squirrel, fox, dove and even crow. Children took buckets into the forest and gathered wild berries and nuts.

Traders, entertainers, clothing salesmen and peddlers traveled through town every season offering their wares for profit. Business was good this year and Christmas was looking to be quite the bounty. Folks were excited.

Three miles above the town, men labored in the mine which opened five years ago by Jakob Mueller, an immigrant from Trier, Germany. Mueller didn't live in Tahosa. He spent most of his time hundreds of miles away in Denver. He was a wealthy investor in Colorado's silver and copper mining ventures and enjoyed the lavish social life Denver had to offer. He visited Tahosa about once every year.

His two sons, Johann and Erick ran the venture in his stead. It wasn't until the strange phenomenon that overtook the town in the weeks to come that Mueller would return confused, grief stricken and at a financial loss.

THREE

GEORGE MCQUIRVING ARRIVED back in Tahosa not long after dark. He now realized how exhausted he really was. He wasn't going to let that deter him from tonight's plans, however. He tied Felix to a tree and kissed him on the nose. Felix nuzzled his owner with a slobbery cuddle. George entered his tent, lit the lantern and pulled out a bottle of whiskey from under the cot and took a long drink. He was filthy. His white shirt was almost black with mud and dirt except for the light, purple smear on his left sleeve. *Must've brushed that damned wagon*, he thought. George walked outside, filled a bucket from the river and went back into his tent to wash up.

About twenty minutes later, his friend, Father Kettling came to visit.

"George", he croaked.

"Hi Paul", George replied. "Staying dry?"

"Nope!" replied the priest as he grabbed the bottle and gulped. They both chuckled at the joke.

"Hey Paul, have you met Millie Orman, that gal who does the dress fixing and such? She moved in around here a few weeks ago".

"Yep. Mighty fine, that one."

Father Paul Kettling was a human being, after all. He was a man very devoted to his profession and would, under no circumstances do anything to disrupt the vows he had taken, but he wasn't dead and appreciated a fine looking woman when he saw one.

"She's been to Mass a couple of times and I've seen her in Ed and Amy's place. You on the hunt,

Georg-o?".

"Little bit, I guess" he said with a smile.

"Nobody ever said you had bad taste, you ole sonofabitch", replied the priest.

"Well, I'm gonna head out and try to find her. Maybe she'll let this old s.o.b. buy her a drink".

"Alright then, good luck. I'll catch up with you in Marck's place".

"Very well. Hey, Paul, where's that monster of a wagon that came in awhile ago? He came down that hill from the Mueller behind me & passed. Not a real friendly feller".

"Wagon? I haven't seen any newcomers in days".

"He's around here somewhere. He rolled in ahead of me".

"Nope, not that I seen".

George stuck his head out of the tent and looked around and toward town. It was dark, but there wasn't anything resembling the visitor or his wagon. "He's around here somewhere. A monk or something. Big, kinda purple colored wagon. Covered wagon, real big. Hmm…. Ok then, see ya in a bit, Paul".

Father Kettling strutted out of the tent toward the saloon.

FOUR

LATER, GEORGE ENTERED Marck's Saloon, eye level,
right into the side of a black man's Winchester rifle barrel. At the end of the man's gun was a young miner he
knew from work. They both looked at George. The room was
full and quiet as a church. All were watching.

It wasn't very often that somebody pulled a gun on a man
or even got into a brawl, but this disgruntled gentleman was
obviously more than agitated. He looked back at the miner at
the end of his gun and screamed "Well, let's hear it! You think
you scare us?!" The miner was speechless. He held his hands up
and shook his head, yelling back "No!.... I don't know! What
the hell do you want?"

"Liar! You've had it out for us ever since we gots here!"
hollered the black man. "Now you pull this! Not anymore, boy!
Time you learned a lesson and leave folks alone!"

The miner looked to George for any kind of help and
George did his best to calmly address the situation.

"Uh, um… okay, men. It's Saturday night and I came here
to have a drink and relax. My bones are cold and sore from
digging all day and I'll be damned straight to hell if I'm gonna
let you boys ruin my night. What we're gonna do is ask nicely
if one of these tables will clear out for a few minutes then sit
down so I can buy us a round. Then we'll talk nice".

The black man's eyes grew wider and angrier as he stared at George and was about to say something when Ely Whitaker entered.

"What the hell?" asked Ely in his deep, gravely voice. George stepped out of the way as the nearest table cleared. The black man replied, "Judge, he done it again. Really bad this time! He keep on a razzin me 'n mine! This time it ends! I don't want to shoot him, but if that's the only way he gonna leave us alone, all the better!"

"Nobody's gonna shoot anybody. Put that thing down!" demanded Ely. The man lowered his gun but kept it loosely pointed at the terrified miner's gut.

"Down, put it down! Sit down, all o' ye" the judge repeated. The man lowered his gun and they all sat, including George.

"How are you involved in this nonsense?" asked Ely. George just shrugged and shook his head.

"I ain't", he replied.

"Then go the hell away!" George stood up and walked over to the bar where he saw Millie Orman. He smiled at her and she nodded politely.

The black man's name was Asa Helms, farmer and rancher. He was thirty four years old and his father had died fighting for the North in the Civil War. He lived peacefully with his fifteen year old daughter, Eva on their small homestead not far out of town. His wife had died four years ago from pneumonia.

The man sprouting from the end of his rifle a few minutes before was nineteen year old Josh Adams. Adams was just a young punk, smart aleck kid who got his kicks harassing Asa and his daughter along with a number of other folks in town- blacks, whites, Indians, Chinese, Irish, Jew. It didn't matter.

Once he put a sign that said "dinner" around a pig's neck and put it in a Jewish family's front yard knowing full well they didn't eat pork. He was, without a doubt a real jackass.

Even as racist as he was, Adams tried to bed Eva more than once. Eva told her father of the advances and made it clear that he was to keep away from them or else. Josh didn't listen and resented the threat. She kept her back to Josh and the kid tried harder to get her attention by making their lives even more miserable. Apparently that's all he knew how to do.

Finally, it was tonight that Asa would speak up and take action. The blood red cross painted on his front door was the last damned straw and that piece of shit, Adams was going to pay for it, one way or another.

As Ely, Adams and Asa began to go over their stories, everyone in the bar went back to enjoying their evenings. Harley started to play and a couple of folks tossed a coin or two into his beer mug.

Ely spoke to both men calmly and at length. He warned Josh that the next time he did anything to anybody he would be locked up. In the meantime, he was sentenced to paint Asa's door and was told to stay away from them. Josh denied the vandalism outright. He didn't necessarily have a problem with his sentence but he pronounced his innocence vehemently.

In turn, Asa was warned that the next time he walked into a public place and threatened anyone like that again he'd face serious charges. Asa nodded in understanding. When he stood up, it caught everyone's attention one last time. It was hard not to see the sadness in his eyes as he glanced around the room before he left.

After the meeting, Ely walked over to George who was speaking casually to Millie. They seemed to be getting along. She was obviously flirting with him and vice versa.

"Miss Orman, George. I don't mean to interrupt, but I think you did a good thing back there. Asa was frosted up enough to use that thing on somebody. Thought it was gonna be you for a second, George".

"So did I", came the reply.

"Well, he didn't. So now, buy me that drink!" Millie chimed in.

"You got it, darlin'!" said George cheerfully.

George yelled to Kevin who was helping his dad behind the bar. Kevin brought over beers for Millie and George and a whiskey for Ely.

"Well, Ely, none of us expected to have to go to court tonight" George said with a nervous laugh.

"I don't think he did it" Ely said quietly. "Wasn't like Josh".

"Hell he didn't. That boy has a mean streak and he'll do anything to get somebody's goat. He only stopped short of burning a cross in that man's yard today. You know his past, pure evil, that kid. Just seems to hate everybody".

Ely thought for a moment and said, "Yeah, I've seen it all. This was hateful and up there with some of the worst things he done, but those other times he was smug, almost proud of making somebody miserable. This time he really seemed upset and denied the whole thing. He said he couldn't really prove it but insisted he was innocent. Even said he'd swear on the Bible if he had to. Watching Asa listen to the boy I think *he* may even have his doubts. Just wasn't like Josh, really".

"Well" George replied "Seems it don't matter much now. Case closed, right?"

"Yup, case closed. Now, shut up, both of you. Time for a party! Dance with me, you old dirt-digger!" Millie said with a smile and grabbed George's hand. They sauntered over to attempt a dance at Harley's less than adequate playing.

Back home, for the first time since his wife died, Asa put his face in his hands at his table and cried.

He didn't just cry, he sobbed. He came to Tahosa to try and get away from this kind of thing and live as a man has a right to. Now he'd been violated and frightened in what he thought was his safe haven. He took the sign as a flat out threat. His father fought and died for his family's freedom and right now it felt just as clear as when Asa was a boy that not a God damned thing had changed. Right now he hated the town, he especially hated Josh Adams.

Once he began to compose himself, he grabbed a wet rag and tried in vain to scrub the hateful message off of the front door. He took a deep breath and started to feel a little better and began to reflect. He thought about how most of the people in Tahosa welcomed him years ago when he first brought his little girl to the tiny town for a new beginning. Father Kettling put him and Eva up in the church until a proper shelter could be built. Ely opened up a line of credit for him at the trading post and that first summer many in the town came together and helped build his little cabin. Once it was complete Ed and Amy Peckman hosted a cookout on his new property.

Over time he bought seeds and livestock and set up shop.

As he thought about these things, he felt a little less angry. Not everybody in the town was as accommodating as Ely, Father Kettling and the Peckmans. Still, he found new opportunity in life and knew he was among mostly friends.

He took to heart what Ely had told him in the bar earlier, that he was a good man and that people like Josh would be dealt a proper fate in good time. Asa knew he was the better man and felt a little embarrassed for letting his temper get so out of control. On the other hand, the punk deserved it and he'd definitely made a point.

Still, as he thought about the conference with Judge Ely and Josh, he couldn't help but feel that there was more to the story. Josh didn't have that look of smug arrogance he'd seen before on the kid's face. This time Josh looked different. He looked almost afraid. A man can protest too much and try too hard to seem innocent, but this didn't seem to be the case. Josh seemed genuine this time. Asa didn't have any reason to believe otherwise, but he began to entertain the notion that maybe someone else had done this. Why? He certainly wasn't the only black man in town.

He glanced over at his sleeping daughter and smiled a little. He got thrown a ringer tonight but he expected that was the end of it.

Far up the river, a faint pale-purplish lantern glowed briefly and faded away into the night.

FIVE

T HE FOLLOWING MONDAY morning the silver miners finished their coffee and breakfasts and began to trickle up toward the mine. Josh Adams was one of the first to head out. For the first time he actually looked forward to going to work and get away from everybody after the previous Saturday night's unpleasant events. He'd kept mostly to himself on Sunday.

He dreaded having to go paint that door after his shift ended that day. He cringed at the thought. He hadn't even seen the ugly mark yet!

He knew he had a bad rap in town but he didn't do this. Damn the nigger for accusing him anyway. *The bastard probably did it himself*, he thought. Just to make an excuse to keep him away from his girl.

Josh knew he liked Eva. Actually, he thought he might even love her. He wasn't about to tell anybody that he had eyes for a darkie, but damned if he didn't dream of her. He snuck a glance her way whenever he could. If she locked eyes with him she quickly turned away as though she'd seen the devil himself. He had no idea what to do, how to approach her, nothing. He wanted to talk to her, hold her, kiss her and tell her what she meant to him, that he wasn't all that bad, etc. It hurt him to know that now she probably hated him more than ever. He'd never have a chance to try and make things right.

He thought for a long time. He was almost to the mine and figured that Asa more than likely did not paint that mark himself. That would just be stupid. Nonetheless, Josh was, without a doubt angry at the accusation. Who could have done it? He decided that maybe he should try to talk to Eva. He hoped she'd be there when he got to her cabin later. At the same time he was afraid of what her reaction would be. He knew Asa had said what he had to say Saturday night. He'd have him paint the door and that would be that.

Then again, maybe he should talk to Asa also. He was innocent and he wanted them to know it. He started to think of what he might say and became flustered. "Hell with it for now", he said to himself. He figured he'd just go do his duty at their cabin after work and try and say what he could.

AMY PECKMAN CLEANED up after the morning's breakfast rush. The rain was gone and the sun was shining on a cool morning. Ed had left to hunt for new items to put on the restaurant's menu. Dr. Stigg always had his coffee in the little establishment and had become good friends with the Peckmans. He was a man of average age and size. He always dressed well and was well spoken with a quick wit.

Father Kettling was working on his breakfast in the far corner reading a two week old newspaper.

Once the miners left and the town folk started their days, the restaurant calmed down considerably until lunch.

Del looked away from his journal and out the window for a moment when he saw it, the huge, dark covered wagon slowly rolling toward them from the direction of the miner's camp. He stood up to get a better look. "It's purple!" he said aloud.

"What d'ya say, Del?" Amy shouted from the kitchen.

"It's purple. That rig is all purple, top to bottom" he answered.

Amy walked over and stood next to him. "Heaven sakes! Haven't seen that one. Just come in?"

All they could see of the driver were two brown gloved hands holding the reigns of the two oxen pulling the monstrosity. The rest of him was shadowed by the darkness of the purple canvas.

Father Kettling overheard them and walked over to get a look for himself. "Oh yeah. You know, George McQuirving mentioned something about a wagon like that the other night. It *is* a big 'un!" he stated.

"Yes, it is" replied the doctor. "George said he saw it before?"

"Yep, Saturday night when he walked home. It rolled in ahead of him. He was asking me about it. I told him I hadn't seen anything like that. Nobody else said anything about it that I know of either".

The wagon turned left and rolled past the restaurant. They watched it creak to a stop in front of the church. Father Kettling walked out the front door and stood on the wooden porch and waited. The other two followed. "George said he thought the driver might be a monk or somethin'. Kinda looks like it. Guess I'd better check it out" the Father said frowning with an exasperated tone. He handed Amy a dime to pay for his meal and walked toward the strange rig.

The rear of the wagon was dark and the priest could not see what was inside. He was astonished at how big it was. The wheels were almost as tall as he was and he was not a short man. He walked cautiously around the side and toward the front. The oxen were standing motionless. The people across the street stopped what they were doing and watched. Time seemed to freeze.

"Hello?" he said. No answer. He walked to the front of the wagon and peered up at the driver. The sun directly above blinded him. Fr. K shielded his eyes and asked, "Can I help you?"

The driver stared down at him. The priest could not see the face, but could tell that the driver was, in fact dressed like a monk. His head was covered with a large hood. He wore a brown friary robe tied with a purple rope at the waist.

The weird visitor tossed a brown paper package tied with a violet ribbon down to the priest who caught it as it thumped his chest, falling into his hands.

"Uh, thanks, friend. I'm Father Kettling, Pastor of Holy Trinity Catholic Church". He waited for a reply as he held up his hand in greeting. The strange friar turned his head forward and snapped the reigns without acknowledging the gesture. The oxen slowly pulled the wagon ahead and began to turn around.

"You got business here, friend? If you have time, I could sure use some help at the church. Plenty of room if you need a place to stay" The driver never so much as looked back. He drove back toward the miner's camp.

Father K. stood in the road somewhat perplexed. He was insulted by the stranger's rudeness. "Hey!" he shouted and jogged after the wagon, stopping short. Suddenly, he felt he should just stay away from that rig and its driver altogether. A feeling of foreboding came over him and a cold, icy chill coursed through his veins. Something was very wrong but he couldn't quite place it. He looked at the people across the street. He sensed they felt it too. He began to sweat some on his forehead and wiped his brow as he looked down at the package.

Everyone watched as the wagon drove on into the thick forest to the right of the camp. There was barely room for a carriage on that particular trail leading up the river, but that crazy friar was going to take it. The wagon disappeared into the thin aspen trees which snapped under its wheels.

Father K. looked down at the package. It was about the size of a shoe box. He wanted to just throw it away, but it might be important. For some reason he dreaded opening it. He realized he was very afraid but had no real reason to be. *Curious,* he thought.

He turned and walked back toward Peckman's place where Amy and the doctor were still standing out front.

"Who is he?" asked Amy.

"I don't know" Father K. replied. "He just threw this at me and drove away".

"Go ahead, open it"

"Uhh, I don't know. I got a strange feeling about this".

"It's obviously for you, Paul. Seeing as a man of the cloth and all delivered it to you *at* the church" said the doctor. "I think you should open it".

"Uh... Alright", he grumbled.

The priest put the package on a table by the door and untied the ribbon. He tore the brown paper off of the thin wooden box and stared down at it. He opened the lid. A small piece of paper with what looked like a poem lay atop its contents. He picked it up and the three examined it. The ink was a dark violet, almost vermillion red written in beautiful calligraphy. Father Kettling read the poem aloud:

> As death embrace,
> Her body graced,
> In this dress,
> She'll lay in state,
> Come the time,
> Sprinkle with lime,
> Behold Tahosa's,
> Woeful sighs
> It begins....

The three stared at each other. Father K.'s hands shook. Amy bit her lip nervously. Dr. Stigg pulled the contents from the box and held it up. It was a beautiful lavender dress.

SEVEN

E LY DID A lot of business at the trading post on Mondays. This morning the place was crowded as usual.

Asa Helms had come in to buy paint and a few supplies before making his rounds.

He and Asa talked and laughed a little bit about the previous Saturday night. They joked about the wide eyed look on George's face, mainly. Ely said it'd probably be a long time before Josh messed with anybody else. Asa agreed.

Ely asked about Eva. "She's doing really good. Growing up so fast, Ely. One of these days she's gonna be on her own".

"I reckon. She sure is a great kid, Asa. You're a lucky man. One of the nicest gals around. You know, I could sure use some help around here" he said, as he glanced at the crowded room. "Why don't you ask Eva if she'd want to work here for a few hours every day? If it's okay with you, 'course. I know you're busy with your own place and all".

Asa smiled and said he thought it was a great idea. He thanked Ely and opened the door to leave when screams from outside sent him running into the street. Ely and his customers followed.

A crowd was beginning to form in front of the small white house a few doors down. Millie Orman had moved in just weeks ago. People were entering and their horror could be heard outside. Ely shoved his way through the crowd and entered the small living room.

A naked Millie was nailed to the wall as if crucified. There were long nails in each palm and one through both feet. A fourth attached her forehead to the wall behind her. She'd been gutted like a deer, her organs were scattered on the floor. A cross was painted in blood over the nail in her head, her facial expression was one of ghastly horror. Her eyes were wide open, her face frozen in a silent scream. Oddly, there was little to no blood.

Ely stood in shock. His horror quickly caught up to him as he felt himself almost fall over. Father Kettling and Dr. Stigg stared in disbelief on either side of him. Del turned and looked at the priest who held the contents of the package he'd opened only moments ago. "Paul", he said. The others in the room watched in silence as the priest held the dress and poem up for Ely's inspection.

Two of Millie's customers had discovered the body when they went to drop off a petticoat for repair.

Ely ordered everyone out. Upon inspection of the house he, Del and Asa discovered Millie's belongings were mostly in order. Her dress and supply inventory was accounted for. Nothing was missing *aside from her heart.*

In the bedroom, her clothing had been folded neatly on the corner of the bed. Atop them was a small purple hanker chiefembroidered with the lettersM O.

Ely questioned Del, Amy and Father. K about the morning's strange delivery. The body was removed and taken to the undertaker. A messenger was recruited to try and contact her family, if she had any.

Ely knew that this town now had a very big problem.

EIGHT

WHEN GEORGE ARRIVED home from work that evening, Father Kettling and a bottle of whiskey were waiting for him. Word had spread quickly. A boy had charged up the hill on horseback after the body was discovered, alerting the miners.

The disturbing news made it difficult for him to work. George felt indescribable sadness and shock. He couldn't say whether he was actually broken hearted but he was terribly upset nonetheless. He and Millie had a great time Saturday night. They decided to attend Mass together the next day and after, Millie made lunch. He'd just met her, for Crissakes!

"George, I...." started Father K.

"It's alright, Paul. We all heard about it this morning. Can't believe it" George said exhaustively. He plopped down on his cot and took a long pull from the bottle offered to him. "After all these years with just Felix to keep me company, I finally met a gal I really like and she's... now...." he trailed off, shaking his head.

"We're going to hold her funeral on Wednesday if you think you can attend. Not too many knew her that well yet. You can say a few words, if you want. I know how much you liked her. Definitely need another pall bearer".

"Yeah, Paul, I'd like that. Thanks".

They talked more about the weird delivery from the wagon driver and the murder. They also talked about what happened to Asa and Eva.

"Asa Helms is pretty shook up too, George. He came to me after they found Millie this morning. He saw that blood mark on her forehead and was beside himself. I think he's scared shitless".

"A'course he is, Paul! I would be too!" George almost yelled. Father K was a bit taken aback and George looked at him apologetically. "Sorry, long day. To tell you the truth, I'm scared". The priest nodded in agreement. "Who the hell does something like this? We need to find that wagon! Ely has already deputized some of us, me included. Some of the men formed a posse and are out looking for him right now. I bet we find him in no time".

The priest took the bottle from George and took a long drink. They didn't feel like hanging around in the tent so they went to the saloon which presented a very somber atmosphere.

NINE

AFTER MIDNIGHT, HARLEY, Kevin, Ed Peckman and four others who'd volunteered for the posse rode back into town. Their search turned up nothing and they were all still wired from the excitement of the day. Stewart Marcks was in the saloon which he kept open all night this night for obvious reasons. There was a loose nut out there and there's safety in numbers. The men dismounted, tied their horses and headed inside. Some folks decided to spend the night in the bar and a few congregated for the night at Holy Trinity.

Father Kettling led his parish in a Rosary at his own suggestion. Many were asleep in their pews by the time it ended. Normally that irritated the hell out of him but not tonight. The priest had made coffee and handed out as many blankets as he could find. Considering his disturbing encounter that morning he did not want to be alone either. He slept under the altar.

TEN

TUESDAY CAME AND went. Millie Orman's body lay in state in her home. She was not dressed in the lavender dress the strange monk had intended for her to wear. Instead she would be buried in a dark green dress she had designed and made herself. A black veil covered the hole in her forehead. Ely posted a guard at the house and people came and went to pay their respects.

Asa and Eva had spent the night in the church with Father Kettling. George stayed in his tent with his 1860 Navy Colt pistol under his pillow. He didn't sleep very well and when he did fall asleep he woke up from a nightmare.

He'd dreamt about the wagon he'd seen on the trail that previous Saturday evening. In the dream, the driver had a face. It was Millie's, distorted and ghastly. George gasped and woke up shivering. In a cold sweat he looked around the dark tent and heard the wind in the pines. He also heard the sound of a wagon creaking past.

He shot up, ran to the tent flaps and stuck his head out into the night air. There was no wagon. He could see the lights from some of the windows in town. Otherwise it seemed like a quiet night. Cold fear gripped him and he sat for some time with his pistol in his hand. He had a couple of drinks hoping it would calm his nerves. It didn't help much.

ELEVEN

EDNESDAY MORNING A modest crowd gathered at the church for Millie's funeral. Father Kettling washed up, shaved and dressed accordingly for a man of his profession. Millie had been brought to the church and she rested in front of the altar in a closed pine coffin.

Millie had been a tiny woman. Only four men served as pall bearers. One of them was, of course George. He had seen her the day before when she laid in state in her home. She looked absolutely beautiful. He remembered how much fun they'd had on their two dates the previous weekend. *Just my damned luck*, he thought. He looked toward the crucifix above the altar and shook his head.

George had a few girlfriends in his time. His relationships usually didn't last long. He had trouble meeting women in the first place, growing nervous and tongue tied when he approached them.

He was definitely not the type of man that could easily meet someone. Millie had been so easy to talk to. She'd told him she'd seen him around and that she thought he was handsome in a "dusty, fuzzy sort of way" whatever that meant. It didn't matter. To him it was music to his ears.

George gave a nice eulogy. Even though he knew her briefly he had a lot to talk about. After Mass, the congregation gathered outside and proceeded to the cemetery.

The Tahosa City Cemetery was located ½ mile to the north east of town. It was sparsely populated with a handful of graves. The small crowd walked behind the makeshift hearse which Ed Peckman drove. They sang a simple hymn as they walked.

Millie was to be placed in the northwest corner of the yard. Several of the town's men and boys dug the grave the day before.

As she was lowered into her final resting place, Father K. blessed the coffin with holy water and read a Prayer for the Deceased. George tossed some flowers he picked on the way onto the coffin.

As Fr. Kettling read aloud, a small boy in attendance yelled "Look!" Everyone turned their heads at once. Atop the plateau above town was parked the mysterious purple wagon. Next to it stood the weird monk as if paying his own demented respects.

Ed jumped into the wagon and Ely shouted for everyone to get back to the saloon and get the posse together. George, Ely and several of the other men jumped into the back of the wagon as Ed snapped the reigns. The horse turned and charged down the hill.

"Who the hell is he, Paul?" shouted Ely to Father Kettling as the wagon sped away. All the priest could do was shake his head.

In town they had seen the intruder on the plateau. Men were already heading up the hill. The rest were saddling up when Ed and his passengers returned. This time they were going to get him! Ely lent a horse to George. Every man was armed. George carried his Navy Colt and Ely preferred a .12 gauge double barrel. Ed, Harley and Kevin checked their Winchester repeaters. So far, the posse had grown to twelve men.

A thirteenth man rode up to meet them with a rifle strapped to his back. Asa Helms was going to defend his town.

The small army charged past the trading post and up the densely wooded hill. Amy looked to the bald top of the rocky plateau and noticed that the big ugly wagon had turned around and was slowly starting to descend down the other side. She could hear the loud snapping of trees as it moved. "How fast could a wagon that size move anyway?" she wondered aloud. "I think they're gonna get 'im".

A woman standing next to her nodded in agreement.

By the time the men reached the plateau, the wagon was gone. They looked down the opposite side of the hill and saw the broken trees left by the path of the monster's escape. Most of the men descended on horseback in pursuit. Ely dismounted and ordered a watch be posted. Kevin, Asa, Harley and two others immediately volunteered. Ely would ride back to town and keep order there while manning his trading post. He was needed and Eva could stay with him for the time being.

TWELVE

MIDST ALL OF the confusion over the last few days, Josh never painted the Helms' door. He had shown up to their cabin Monday night per his orders and saw that it had already been taken care of.

He'd left work early this particular afternoon to try and attend Millie's wake and perhaps offer his assistance in the search for the suspected killer. He was late but noticed Eva across the street. He took a deep breath and walked over to her.

"Hey, Eva. I guess your dad painted the door. I..I come by t'other night to do it but you nor your pa wasn't around. I know you think I done that but I want you to know I didn't. I really didn't. I swear!"

Eva locked eyes with him for a long while as she pursed her lips in anger and narrowed her eyes and said, "All you is is a boy, Josh Adams. You just a little boy with a little pecker. For some reason my daddy think you didn't do it neither. But I think he's wrong".

"I didn't, I swear! I really mean it! I been wantin' to tell you. It was a awful thing, whoever done it. Really awful and mean. I know I done a lot of stupid shit to people, but I'd never do anything to hurt *you*".

"What?" She thought for a moment as she studied him. "What the hell you talkin' about Josh Adams? Since when do you give a mule's ass what I feel?"

He had no idea what to say. What he really wanted to tell her he didn't have the nerve to. He just stared back at her.

"You're a fool! A lyin' fool!" she said and stormed off.

"Eva, wait a minute".

She ran to the trading post.

Josh felt defeated. He walked slowly back to his tent and threw his pack and tools inside. His mind was too full of Eva Helms when he plopped down on his bedding without noticing what lay there.

Beneath him the thick paper crunched. He stood, startled and looked down at a wrapped, brown package tied with a purple ribbon. They'd all heard about the mysterious package Father Kettling had received that previous Monday morning..

Panic gripped him. He ran from his tent, gasping and fell. Some of the other miners outside looked at him quizzically. "Rattler in your bunk, boy?" one asked. They all laughed. He looked back at them wide eyed and shaking. He couldn't speak, he just looked back at his tent.

THIRTEEN

EVA HELPED ELY finish closing up the trading post at the end of the day. They walked down the street to Peckman's Restaurant and he bought them dinner like he promised with a big slice of apple pie each for dessert.

They talked through the whole meal. She asked how he became a judge, when and how he ended up in Tahosa, etc. He explained that he was originally from Kansas and settled in Denver as a teenager with his family.

During the war, Denver was besieged by Indians for a time. That prompted him to join the US Army.

He later worked as a deputy, went to law school, became a lawyer and eventually worked to his title, Justice of the Peace.

"I moved to Tahosa in '74 to be with my brother" he added. "He was sick and ended up dyin' the following year of fever. He's buried up there in the cemetery. The trading post was his originally and it gave me a place to set up as a judge. The settlement needed some sort of law. When he died, I took over the post and kept judgin'. That's about it".

The conversation ended with the matter of Millie Orman's killing.

"You know your pa's probably gonna be out for a few nights, Eva. I deputized him this morning and he's helpin' us see what we can find out about that bastard killer".

"Yes, Mr. Whitaker. My pa told me before he left this mornin'. You think they gonna find that man?"

"Oh, 'course. That dumb, lumbering monk, or whatever he is just got lucky a few times. Won't be long, I reckon. We'll git 'im" he said as he smiled.

"Thanks for dinner Mr. Whitaker".

"Aw, you're welcome Eva. Thanks for helping me out at the post". He sighed. "Well, I'm not quite ready to turn in. I feel like havin' a drink. Mind if we step into the saloon for a bit? If you don't like whiskey or beer, Stewart makes sasparilla and lemonade. Coffee too, if you want".

"I don't mind beer once in awhile. My pa brews and sells some of his to Mr. Marcks' who sells it 'n his establishment".

"No kiddin!"exclaimed Ely. "Well, I guess we know what we're drinkin' then, right?"

She laughed. "Sounds great, Mr. W, thanks again for everything".

"My pleasure".

Ely paid Ed Peckman and they walked down the street to the saloon. Harley could be heard banging away on his piano.

Once inside, Ely sat down to play cards with the locals while Eva sat by the piano and watched Harley. She loved music and watched him whenever she could. She especially enjoyed it when Kevin sat in with him. She thought Kevin was a pretty good banjo player, much better than Harley was at piano. But, Harley was getting better, sort of. At least he was starting to learn a few more songs. She tossed a penny into the musician's mug and went and sat at the bar.

After losing one too many rounds of poker, Ely left the game, walked over and sat down next to her and ordered a whiskey.

Josh Adams, who'd spent the remainder of the afternoon alone and scared to death walked in the door. He held the contents of the package he'd been left– another poem and a new black suit.

Wide eyed, he looked around the room and saw Ely sitting next to Eva at the corner of the bar. She was laughing at something Ely said.

Josh swallowed hard and almost turned around and left. He had to talk to Ely, though. He walked timidly up to them.

"Pardon me, Judge Whitaker" he said. Eva's smile vanished in a flash. She frowned and turned away.

"Howdy Josh. What can I do for you?" The boy's face was pale and he looked frightened. Ely looked at him concerned and said, "Stewart, I think Josh here could use a belt. Set him up for me, would you?" Stewart poured a generous amount of whiskey into a glass and slid it to Ely.

"Here son, you look like you need it".

Josh nodded, gulped the whiskey down and grimaced.

"Sir, somebody left this on my cot" he said and handed the suit and the poem over.

Ely read the poem silently.

> As death embrace,
> His body graced,
> In this suit,
> He'll lay in state,
> Come the time,
> Sprinkle with lime,
> Behold Tahosa's,
> Woeful sighs
> It continues....

Ely's mouth went dry and he stared at the items. He looked back at Josh. Eva turned back around to see what was transpiring. The judge cleared his throat. "Josh, tell me what happened. These were in your tent?"

"Yessir. I come home and it was all wrapped up on my beddin'. This was tied around it". He produced a purple ribbon from his pocket. Eva covered her mouth and gasped.

"You share a tent with anybody else?" said Ely.

"Yessir, two others. We all work the mine".

"Anybody see anything or anybody else go into your tent?"

"No sir. I thought it was t'others who was just pullin' one over on me. Don't really think they did, though".

"Well… " Ely thought for a moment. "Josh. You gotta understand you've done a lot of foolish things around here. You ain't the most popular man in town, you know. I wouldn't doubt if somebody *was* trying to pull a fast one on you".

Josh looked at Eva who said, "Don't look at me, Josh Adams. I was runnin' errands for Mr. Whitaker here all day long. I ain't even gonna take time to mess with you. You ain't worth it".

Josh shook his head. "I don't think it was you, Eva".

Ely instructed the girl to stay in the saloon and walked with Josh to his tent. They could see the fire far atop the plateau where the posted watch was holding vigil.

Inquiries in the miners' camp yielded no results. He instructed them all to keep an eye out for each other and suggested night watchmen for the area. They agreed and decided to sleep in shifts.

FOURTEEN

THE FOLLOWING FRIDAY morning, Ely was told of a second murder and raced to the mine where the body had been discovered.

At the mine entrance, Jakob Mueller's twenty eight year old son, Johann, the eldest of his two boys and chief foreman of the mine hung by his neck, dead. He was naked. His own intestines served as his noose and were attached to a pine bough fifty feet above.

There was a red cross in blood marked on his forehead. His penis had been removed and was knotted around his exposed windpipe (presumably to mimic some perverse form of necktie). His internal organs had been scattered high in the trees and on the ground. Again, there was little blood. Later, a search would tell of his missing heart.

Josh Adams had fainted immediately upon discovering his dead employer. Other miners mounted up and rode back to town for help.

Josh now sat far down the trail staring numbly at nothing in particular. Unreasonable guilt plagued him. He knew there was no way he could have known what would happen. After all, he thought he would be the one to be murdered. He was the one the foreboding package had been left for two days before.

The victim's brother, Erick was sitting on the ground wailing in despair not far away. Several folks had offered him whiskey and tried to comfort him as best as possible but the man was overtaken with grief.

The dead man's wife became hysterical upon arrival and was led away immediately.

Ely and Ed checked the mine office and found the victim's clothes neatly folded on his desk along with a folded purple hanker chief atop them, just like Millie's. This time, the hanker chief was embroidered with the letters, JM.

Once again, nothing was missing or out of place.

A few miles away, the posse readied to leave camp. They were not yet aware that another gruesome murder had taken place.

FIFTEEN

Twelve miles upriver the purple wagon rolled slowly through a small Ute camp. The residents silently watched and moved out of its way as others peered out of their homes. The monk stared straight ahead, oblivious to those around him.

SIXTEEN

S ATURDAY AFTERNOON, FATHER Kettling returned to the cemetery. He had been planning Johann Mueller's funeral Mass which would be held the following morning.

He told the two men digging the grave to take a break and come down to the church for some coffee and pie. One of the men pulled out a flask of whiskey and Fr. K and the other man were more than happy to help themselves.

As they started down the hill, the priest glanced sideways toward the corner of the cemetery yard. "Boys, you head on down" he said. "I'll be along in a minute" He walked over to Millie Orman's grave. On the mound, a purple hanker chief lay folded beneath a human heart.

SEVENTEEN

THE FULL POSSE and other town residents congregated at the saloon for a meeting. It was agreed that the posse would split up into teams of two and three. George and Ed Peckman would ride west together up river past the miner's camp. Several Indians had also volunteered to join the search and lead a larger posse of their own, traveling southward toward other Indian encampments.

Asa felt compelled at this point to stay in town with his daughter. He wanted to protect her as much as possible; and he had a ranch to run.

Suddenly, Father K burst into the room. The heart he'd found was in his hands, wrapped in the purple cloth. He was wide eyed with a look of terror on his face. He held it up for all to see. The others stared in disbelief and everyone began talking, pointing and yelling, mainly at Ely. Stewart Marcks banged on the bar with the club he kept for protection.

"Shut up! Shut up! Shut up! All 'o ya!" he yelled. The man was huge and had a booming deep voice. He handed the club to Ely. "You're the judge, now judge. The rest of you shut the hell up! Can't even think!"

The room fell silent and Ely nodded to Father K who told the room about what he'd found.

There was silence for a moment then a man spoke up.

"What's going on here, Father? Seems to me this all points back to you somehow" The room erupted again. Ely banged the club gavel on a table and restored order.

"Nobody's gonna accuse nobody of nuthin' in this room!" Ely said. "How in the hell you could come up with a connection like that I'll never understand! You know as well as I do that the only suspect we got here is that nut job out ridin' around foolin' all o' your dumb asses!" He looked back at the priest who stood shocked at what he'd just been asked. "Paul, sit down. We're all just on edge here. There's something going on that's pure evil and we need your help." Most in the room nodded in agreement.

Another voice spoke up from the crowd. "Father, nobody thinks you done nuthin'. But, you talked to that bastard up close. What'd he say? What's he look like? Have you seen 'im before?"

"I saw him up close….*and*, I talked to him" George added as he stood. "He don't say anythin'. He just looks at you but you can't tell what he looks like with that damn hood over 'im. It's the most unsettlin' thing I ever saw."

After the meeting, the men filtered back outside and began stocking up with supplies. The Indians were the first to set out. Men rode out in their assigned teams and

George and Ed saddled up and headed for the river.

EIGHTEEN

SA AND EVA returned to their ranch that afternoon. Eva worked at the stove warming up a pie they had bought from Peckman's. She and her father would take it to the Mueller home that afternoon when they paid their respects to the family. Asa wrapped up some light work outside.

The ranch was only five acres and he thought about the Muellers who frequently rode through on their way to and from town often stopping to chat or just wave hello in passing. They were some of his best customers and he found them all to be very likeable. He even considered them friends to some degree.

After he made his rounds, Asa and his daughter began to get cleaned up for their visit to the Mueller home. Eva wore a dress that had been owned by her mother. It was still as beautiful as the day it was bought. Asa wore his nice boots, black coat, tie and derby hat. Together they left on foot.

The Mueller mansion was abuzz with folks coming and going. Johann Mueller looked noble in his best suit as he lay in state. The undertaker had done a lovely job on him. He wasn't made up too much and his hair was neatly combed. He was, of course not clothed in the monk's gift attire.

Mrs. Mueller looked completely exhausted and devastated but smiled and greeted everyone warmly. Her brother in law, Erick drank whiskey and chatted with other men in the parlor.

Asa and Eva entered the grand front room in front of the stair case where Mrs. Mueller greeted and hugged them. She held Asa tightly for a long time and wiped a tear away. She thanked them for the pie and led Asa into the parlor where Erick greeted him with a smile, a hand shake and offered him a drink. "Oh, yes, whiskey at the Mueller home—the best around when we all really need it", Asa said. Erick and the other gentlemen erupted in laughter.

The mood was light in the home. Eva went over to the grand piano in the adjoining sitting room and quietly played what little Harley had taught her. She wished she had a piano. Mrs. Mueller heard her playing and came in to visit.

"My husband played effery day" she said in her thick German accent as she sat down next to her guest. "He vas really good actually but didn't like to play in front of people. Not even me. Sometimes he'd catch me listening from zee ozzer room and he'd just stop completely". She laughed. Eva smiled.

"I love playing. Harley at the saloon taught me a little but he don't play all that well so he probably ain't a very good teacher neither", Eva replied.

Mrs. Mueller laughed and said "Vell, I guess we all have to zshtart learning somehow, right?"

Eva told her how she'd always wanted a piano and that the only time she got to play was at the saloon when it wasn't crowded. "Vell, we might have to zee if there's zomesink vee can do about zat" Mrs. Mueller replied. "You're velcome any time, Eva. It'd be nice to have zomebody put zis old sing to use. Dat is, as long as you let me listen" she said smiling. Eva agreed and properly thanked her. Her host walked back into the living room.

The men in the parlor continued drinking and laughing. Many of them were Asa's customers. Some were investors in his little ranch.

Josh Adams walked into the house to pay his respects. He stared at the body in the coffin for a long while. Asa spotted him, excused himself from the parlor and approached him. "Josh" he said.

"Afternoon, Mr. Helms". Josh stared at the floor unable to make eye contact.

"I took care of that door. Don't worry 'bout that no more. I know you didn't have nothin' to do with that. You're mean but I don't think you're that mean".

"Nossir, I ain't. I feel bad for other stuff I done, though. 'specially 'cause I know Eva thinks I'm the devil".

Asa laughed. "Oh, for cryin' out loud, boy she don't think you're the devil. She just thinks you a jackass. She's in the other room messin' round on the piano. Go on. Go talk to her if you feel the need. Tell her I told her to be nice. But, you watch y'self. Got my eye on you".

"Uh, maybe, okay. Thanks, Mr. Helms".

He walked into the sitting room and leaned on the piano. Eva stopped playing when she saw him enter and she immediately spoke to him. "Josh Adams, now what you want?"

"Nuthin'. You're pa told me I could come talk to you and you're supposed to be nice to me" he replied.

"What? Why? Why you want to talk to me?" she said defiantly.

"Just do." He looked around the room.

She looked in the other room and saw her dad watching.

"Fine. Talk."

"Um, okay. I uh....see, I feel real bad about the stupid stuff I done".

"Why?"

"'cause I do! Look, I know my whole life I been like that".

"Like what, a dimwit?"

"Hey, I ain't stupid!"

"Sure act stupid sometimes"

"Well, I don't want to anymore..uh, act mean, I mean, not... not stupid". He was getting flustered and took a breath and paused. "Dammit! I don't want you to hate me, that's all. I know nobody really likes me 'cause I do so much stupid stuff but I'm getting' tired of it. Been on my own since my pa died and all I do is work in that mine from sun up to sun down. I'm tryin' to be nice. See, I… well… okay.… I, I think you're the prettiest girl I ever seen and I wanna talk to you. A lot."

He did it. He said it. Eva stared at him with her mouth open, speechless. Josh looked at her wide eyed and startled, mumbled something and turned and quickly walked out of the room. He walked past Asa who watched him run out the door and down the road toward town. He looked back to his daughter who still sat at the piano. With a startled look on her face she got up and walked over to her dad. "Fool boy" she said. Asa shrugged and they went to join the others who'd gone out back to eat.

NINETEEN

T HAT EVENING AFTER the dinner rush, Amy Peckman closed up the restaurant for the day. She felt safe knowing that Dr. Stigg lived in the other apartment while her husband was away. Del had left his coat in the restaurant that afternoon and she figured she'd just return it before retiring. She took off her apron, walked into the adjoining hallway and knocked on Del's door. There was no answer. She knocked again. "Del?" she said, noticing a faint light growing brighter under the door. She knocked a third time. "D—"

The door swung open, loudly slamming into the wall behind it. The monk stood just inside the doctor's apartment holding a lantern which emitted a deep bluish glow. He stood just inches from her.

Amy stumbled backwards and screamed. Gasping, she turned and ran as fast as she could down the hallway, out the front door and down the street to Ely's house. She pounded desperately on his window and a startled Ely answered. Amy was hysterical! She couldn't speak but pointed toward her restaurant. Ely grabbed his shotgun and ran. Peering around the corner of the building, gun at the ready he cautiously entered the rear door. "Hello? Del?" he cried. "Del? You in here? Anybody here?" There was no answer.

Others heard the commotion and went to investigate. Ely carefully opened the doctor's door. The apartment was empty. Nothing seemed out of order, but this late it was unusual for Del to be out. Normally he retired to his rooms by 7:00 or so. It was now well past nine.

TWENTY

EORGE AND ED made camp for the night ten miles up-river. They'd encountered no one in the day's search. They were a little over two miles from the next Indian encampment and in the morning they would inquire there. They drank some whiskey and ate some jerky, biscuits and apples. Ed was famished and ate like a horse. He was also dead tired and crawled into their tent, falling asleep almost immediately. George stayed up awhile longer and drank a few more slugs of whiskey. He could hear coyotes howling in the distance as Ed snored loudly.

George finally settled in and laid down. He was tired but not really sleepy. He lay on his back staring at the ceiling for a long time. Eventually sleep came and again, he dreamt.

This time, George dreamt of the mine. He was lost inside. Although he knew the Mueller like the back of his hand, he could not find an exit. Every tunnel led to another tunnel which morphed into yet another. He began to panic and started to run. The lantern he was carrying was beginning to dim which was a very bad sign. He began to feel short of breath, nauseas and dizzy. *I have to calm down* he thought.

The lantern flame vanished. Turning around he noticed light far down the tunnel. He started walking quickly toward it. Getting closer, he began to breathe easier. He could see the silhouette of a man sitting against the wall about one hundred yards ahead. George sprinted to him.

The man had is back to the wall and looked terrified. He was hugging his knees to his chest and was breathing quickly and heavily. George recognized him as the doctor who had stitched up his arm from a nasty cut months ago. George had slipped in the mine and fell on a jagged piece of ore cart track. It penetrated his right forearm but did no major damage. Faint numbness was still present in two of his fingers but the hand worked normally.

"Doctor Stigg?" George said. The man looked up at him and replied, "I can't get out. It won't let me."

"It?" asked George.

"The mine. It won't let me out. I've tried and I've tried and no matter what I do, I can't find the way out". The doctor began to cry.

"I'm stuck in here too but we'll get out" George said thoughtfully. "I know this mine. t'ain't no reason we stay stuck in here. We'll find the entrance. Don't worry, c'mon".

Del stood with George's help and they began searching for the entrance. The doctor spoke, "We'll all end up here. You know that, don't ya? He'll bring us all here... every last one of us".

George woke up, startled. It was a hot morning and the sun was shining. Ed was outside making some breakfast and drinking coffee when George crawled out of the tent, sat and pulled on his boots. Ed was in good spirits. He hadn't slept that well in weeks.

"George! How are ya? Sleep good?"

"Slept alright. Bad dream though".

George told his friend about the dream as they finished their coffee, packed up and headed toward the Ute Indian camp not far up river.

When they arrived, the Indians were welcoming. It helped that most of them spoke English.

The Utes said they knew about the horrible murders; and that the monk was a wanted man. They were also aware of the Indian posse that had departed to the south the day before. A fellow tribe member staying in town had ridden out to their camp early this morning to report a man was missing, but didn't know who he was.

The people described how the monk had ridden right through their camp days before. He didn't look at anyone or say anything. They felt compelled to just leave him be at the time, but knowing full well he was wanted they would shoot him on sight if they saw him again. George said that it would probably be best if they tried to capture him alive but the Indians unanimously disagreed. "He's a bad man, full of evil spirits. He must be killed" one of them said. George and Ed didn't entirely disagree, of course. "Well, do what you must. It might be for the best" Ed stated.

The two men thanked the people and mounted their horses and continued up river, the direction they were told the monk had come from.

TWENTY ONE

Sunday, September 13, 1882.

SEVERAL MEN, ELY and Amy stayed overnight at Peckman's Restaurant. Dr. Stigg never came home. Father K held the funeral for Johann Mueller as planned that morning, the biggest funeral in the little town's history. Readings were read by Asa Helms and various employees of the Mueller Silver Mine and Johann's brother, Erick said the eulogy.

After the funeral Mass the coffin was wheeled up to the cemetery in the back of a large, expensive glossy black wagon which had been painted for the occasion. Father K performed his rites and Johann Mueller was laid to rest.

The monk made no appearance.

After the funeral, Peckman's Restaurant became busy as usual. Seeing as Ed was out hunting for the killer, Amy had her hands full. Eva Helms and other folks helped out as best they could. The rush helped Amy keep her mind off of Del's disappearance and the frightening encounter she had the night before.

Word had spread about her experience and she was asked about the monk by nearly everybody. *Did she see his face? How tall was he? Is he fat, skinny or medium? Did he have a weapon? Did he speak?* etc. She could only really answer three of the questions: He was about her height, maybe an inch or two taller (she was 5'4") and maybe had a medium build; and he didn't speak.

As folks began to clear out of the restaurant, most went to their homes. Some went to the saloon where Ely manned the search operation. The trading post was closed on Sundays.

Amy and her assistants closed for the day. She needed rest and wanted Ed to come home.

PART II

TWENTY TWO

EORGE AND ED'S search that day had yielded nothing, other than a black bear which was easily scared away by a pistol shot to the ground. They had travelled almost twenty miles to the northeast and back, speaking to anyone who may have come in contact with the accused killer. Finally, at sundown they made camp and built a large fire.

It was not long after supper as George dozed off and Ed poked at the fire when the huge purple wagon rolled in out of nowhere. It stopped a mere twenty yards away. Startled, Ed tried to get to his feet. George opened his eyes and sat, staring in disbelief at the unexpected visitor.

The oxen huffed loudly as the driver stared down at the men. Ed grabbed his rifle and George, already having drawn, stood. They fixed their weapons on the seated monk.

"Throw your hands up!" George demanded. "Get down from there, now!"

"Move!" Ed added.

The monk did not budge. It was as if he was daring them to shoot. It occurred to both men that they really hadn't discussed what the hell they would do if they encountered him. "Get down, now! Now!" Ed ordered. The monk tilted his head back and the firelight revealed part of his face. They couldn't definitively make out the features, but the nose seemed straight and the chin looked unshaven. They saw the shadow of his eyes, black with thin silver beams emitting from them like lasers. Both men felt overwhelming terror rise quickly within them.

The wagon lunged ten feet and stopped. Startled, the men took a step back. The oxen, towering at an unheard of six feet at the forehead huffed loudly, steam bellowing from their wet nostrils. The forest became completely still. Howling coyotes heard in the distance ceased. The wind in the trees made no sound.

The oxen, clearly agitated stomped their hooves with thundering force, rearing their heads angrily from side to side, all the while huffing and groaning. The men could feel the earth tremble under their feet.

George turned to the side and looked at Ed who stood in total fear, his rifle barrel shaking nervously. George returned his stare back toward the driver, aimed his pistol with both hands and again, issued the command to step down. The monk, again ignored him

"Aim at his heart, Ed." George instructed.

"I....I...." Ed shakily replied.

"Do it! You have the rifle!" Ed remained motionless, wide eyed with terror. "Ed! C'mon! Shoot!"

Finally, wasting no time, George aimed and fired. Ed snapped out of his trance and immediately followed, firing twice.

The driver jerked to the side from the impact of the bullets, quickly corrected himself and snapped the reigns. The oxen grunted loudly and the wagon charged the men with shocking speed. George dove out of the way and rolled into the trees. Ed, standing strong, managed another shot before the oxen slammed into him like a locomotive. He was thrown off of his feet and landed flat on is back with a thud. The oxen halted at their master's command and stood right on top of Ed.

One hoof pinned his shoulder to the ground and with a grunt, the oxen violently stomped their huge legs in place, completely macerating the man, killing him.

Again, the monk snapped the reins and the rig rocketed forward for a second time, its two left wheels violating anything left of Ed's remains.

George lay on the ground, watching in horror.

The wagon continued directly into the fire which was thrown in all directions. Dead grass and pine immediately ignited and began to rapidly spread.

The monk stopped and stared down at George. George was terrified but managed to aim his gun and fire three more shots. The monk was clearly hit by two of them. He jerked once from a hit to the upper chest. A second bullet tore into his robes, midsection. He did not fall. He calmly turned away and looked straight ahead. He prodded his oxen forward and the wagon slowly creaked away into the trees, out of sight.

George stood, dumbfounded as he looked around at the rapidly spreading fire. Ed's corpse was now burning. He tried in vain to douse the body with dirt but the smoke and the flames around him were becoming too dangerous. The wind picked up and seemed to circle George like a cyclone. Fire spiraled into the sky. An instant of bright purplish light flashed from the direction the monk had departed.

Before he even had time to react, the fire spread as if fed by kerosene. There was nothing he could do. He had to leave now! He would also have to leave his friend.

George untied the frightened horses which were bucking and whinnying noisily. He swatted Ed's on its behind and it bolted into the trees. He managed to calm his own horse enough to mount. He did not run it for fear of injury to both of them in the thick, dark woods. They trotted away back towards town.

Behind him the fire began to rage.

From a distance, the few folks in Tahosa who were awake could see the growing glow of fire in the night sky. Many began to congregate in the street. Some had heard faint shots earlier. Ely had been awakened and was summoned outside.

"What t'hell?" He said as he watched the distant glow slowly become bigger. The wind was blowing hard in their direction. Ely wasn't entirely sure what to do. He had never had to deal with the kind of crisis that was clearly headed their way. Something had to be done, and fast.

He ordered every able bodied man in town to be awakened and to report to the saloon as soon as possible with every digging and cutting tool available. Picks, axes, saws and shovels were distributed. The Indians across the river began to take down their tepees and prepare for evacuation. Many of them would stay behind to help entrench the town.

There was just enough moonlight to expose the trail back to Tahosa and George and his horse picked up speed. He had outrun the moving fire and could see town far ahead in the distance. He was trying to wrap his mind around what had happened. A lot of windows appeared to be lit and he knew the town had already begun to prepare for the worst. The fire was becoming a deadly wall of destruction behind him. He wondered if he and Ed had made a terrible mistake.

He passed the Indians they had questioned earlier that morning. Their tepees had been dismantled and they were already on the move. They moved to the side of the trail as he trotted by.

He wondered how the hell he was going to tell Amy Peckman about her husband. *At least it was quick* he thought to himself.

He knew he'd shot the monk at least twice. He was pretty sure Ed had also hit him once or twice. It made him feel a little bit avenged for having wounded the killer and wondered if he'd actually fought the monk off in the end or if he'd been spared. He also wondered where that damn wagon had gone.

In town, a small army of three hundred men, women and even children were digging a trench around the perimeter of the settlement. They intended to try and channel the river to create a moat of sorts. Mine storage in the town held dynamite and several controlled blasts nicely started the process.

Dense forest came close to the rear of buildings on either side of the street. These trees were to be cleared as much as possible and moved to the river for damming. The fire looked to be perhaps only a few miles away. Ely was certain they weren't going to make it in time. They were trying to complete a job that could take days in a matter of minutes or hours.

The night sky was aglow with orange and red. Smoke was beginning to block out the full moon above as it drifted into town. Folks were covering their faces with bandanas and other clothing as they worked frantically. They were briefly blessed when the wind changed direction and the fire temporarily blew back on itself. Then the wind seemed to die down altogether. They were still in danger, but by the grace of God they had at least a little more time.

TWENTY THREE

OVER AN HOUR had passed since the fire had started. Trees fell rapidly as they were cut down, one after the other. Felix and other mules were recruited to move the sectioned pines for use to dam the river & create barricades and channels. Others were taken far away. The moat was starting take some form.

The trail had become dark from smoke, making it difficult for George to see. His lungs burned. His progress had been slow but he finally arrived back in town.

Ely and Fr. Kettling were shoveling side by side near the trail when George arrived. He told them about Ed, the monk and how the fire had started. He also explained his inability to recover Ed's body. Father Kettling crossed himself and began to pray softly.

"If you're able, help out here. We sure as hell need it" Ely said to George. "I'll go tell Amy the news. Seems you've had enough grief for one night. You did what you had to do, friend. Any of us would have done the same".

Ely walked briskly between the buildings and into the street toward the restaurant. George could see Amy kneeling as she wiped dirt from a child's face. When Ely reached her she stood. George could see the expression change on her face.

"NO!" She screamed. "Oh, no, no, no!" cried Amy as she collapsed in hysterics, her hands over her face. Ely held her as she cried loudly, gasping in shock and disbelief. George dropped his shovel and ran to her.

"Mrs. Peckman, he didn't feel a thing, honest" he said, his own voice shaking, eyes tearing. "He didn't even know what hit 'im. It happened so fast. I tried to git 'im but I just couldn't. The fire got too big and I just couldn't git 'im! Lord knows I tried". He knelt down beside her. She held Ely tightly as she sobbed.

Again, she cried out and tried to stand. She was completely beside herself. Wide eyed, she stood and scanned her surroundings. Turning, she met George's eyes. Her gaze burned. He wiped a tear from his face and looked down, then up, meeting her eyes. He expected rage and blame. He thought the least he could do was look into her eyes and prepare for the worst.

Several moments passed. She spoke. "How?"

George took a long drink from his flask and explained how the wagon wheeled up to them out of nowhere. He told her the whole story—the shooting, the fire, and of course how valiantly her husband died fighting a killer.

"That damned murderer started that fire!" Ely said. "One missin'. Now three dead! All hell is breakin' loose!"

Amy, shaking and in shock looked around again and began to cry once more. She was devastated and frightened but now she could feel anger taking over. Her husband had been run down like a dog. She thought about how they'd shot the monk. She hoped that son of a bitch would suffer and die slowly, in agony from his wounds. If he didn't, she'd help make sure the job got done.

Digging and the cutting of trees continued. Asa and other farmers in the area plowed deeply enough for the channel to move water from the river into the trench. Its width would be approximately ten feet wide and two to three feet deep. Water began to slowly fill the shallow moat as people dug.

More than three hours had passed since the fire had started just ten miles away. It was now getting close at only three miles. Smoke hung in the little town.

The Indians had worked extremely fast and efficiently to dismantle their tepees and pack their gear.

Those who had chosen to stay helped channel the river. The rest were already gone. They would take refuge at a lake where the river widened farther southeast.

Ely wondered if the project would have any effect at all. He was skeptical. In just over three hours they had managed to dig a channel from the river to possibly help protect the west side of town. It was nearly seventy yards long and the town's only defense.

Buckets were collected and positioned along the filling trench. Buildings would be wetted as much as possible and all were to be at the ready if any part of town were to ignite.

They didn't arrive all at once, but everyone heard the screams and shouts of the injured as they ran into town. They were the Indians George had passed earlier on the trail. Most had dropped what they carried miles back to lighten their load and flee. Many were badly burned and choking from the smoke and ash.

Some tried to swim down river to escape, only to perish in the rapids. Others suffered cracked skulls, broken ribs and limbs, leaving them stranded in the icy, fast rushing water. All they could do was get far away from the flames any way possible.

The fire engulfed much of the region. Father Kettling and others ran to try and help the injured. One young woman collapsed and died in Father Kettling's arms and he prayed aloud, laying her down so he could help others.

George removed his shirt, doused it in water and covered a badly burned little boy. He ran, cradling the boy to the center of town. This area would be the makeshift hospital. Amy and others had gathered blankets and medical supplies. George handed the boy to a woman and ran to find Felix. More hauling was needed.

Horses panicked and bucked, some bolted. Felix stood in place, tied to a stump, whinnying loudly. The man working him had left. Felix's big, brown eyes scouted the scene for any sign of George who finally ran up to his mule and quickly untied him. George hugged him around the neck, kissed him on the snout then mounted and swatted him hard on the backside. Felix didn't move. Another swat and Felix stood motionless, looking straight ahead. "You stubborn....God dammit, go on!" George yelled. He swatted the mule's rump a third time and Felix responded by reaching around and biting George on the foot. George gritted his teeth and rubbed the bite mark. "You son of....I oughtta shoot ya. You know that, right? Fine, go 'head, ya dumb beast, burn up if you want!" George dismounted, turned around and started walking toward the trench. Felix followed.

Ely surveyed his town. The wind picked up and he looked up the mountain in front of him. The fire was now only several hundred yards away and began its attack.

TWENTY FOUR

IGH UP THE mountain the monk was tending to his wounds. He had been shot five times by the vermin miner and his pathetic, squashed and charred friend. He knew he was not going to die. The mere thought amused him. The wound in his stomach would take longer to close, but the wounds in his chest were already beginning to close. There was no blood. That had been taken care of. We'll see why later in the story.

He looked out the rear opening of his huge covered wagon and down at the fire below. He could see the very distant lights in town. He knew what a catastrophe the river and the fire together might cause. It was a delicious thought. The fire would sweep the town. Some would burn to death and the overflowing, routed waterway might drown or trap others. He knew the town population wasn't completely foolish, however. They had, of course dug a canal leading from the channel back to the river to prevent overflowing. The ground would also become weak from the charred earth on the mountainside and undoubtedly cause catastrophic landslides.

He stuck his dagger into his chest and dug around in one of the holes to expel the lodged bullet.

The pain was very slight. He tried to exacerbate it just so he could feel something. He looked back toward the doomed town and smiled slightly.

From outside, the wagon's canopy glowed pale and purple. The killer continued to probe his wounds.

TWENTY FIVE

SOME IN THE settlement had decided to evacuate. Most stayed. The nearest town was miles away and there was the fear that any escape route might end up right in the path of the fire.

Smoke poured into the settlement and the heat from the fire was stifling. Flames shot fifty feet or more into the air. Sparks and embers blew into the street and onto buildings. Some jumped into the trench. Others took their chances by running to the river.

Water was poured onto the injured and those treating them. People ran to and from buildings, dousing them as much as possible. Bed sheets, curtains and canopies were soaked and hung as makeshift tents.

Mrs. Mueller, Erick and their servants had packed up and fled to town. On the way they stopped briefly at the Helms' place. Asa and Eva were clearly in town already or had evacuated entirely. Erick freed Asa's small herd of cattle as his sister in law looked up the trail and watched her grand home burn to the ground.

Ironically, the first building in town to go up in flames had been Millie Orman's house. A burning ember flew onto the roof, the dry wood catching immediately. A bucket line was formed and even though men worked quickly the house was consumed and destroyed in a matter of minutes, taking the house next door with it. Like falling dominoes, a third structure caught fire- *the saloon.*

"Oh, like hell!" Stewart Marcks hollered as he grabbed a bucket and ran to his building. Harley, Kevin, Asa and Father Kettling removed their shirts, soaked them and began beating at the flames. Harley grabbed an axe, rushed inside and began an attempt to chop down the flaming south wall. Ten other men including Asa and George also grabbed axes and ran inside to help.

A second bucket line stretched into the building. This helped to douse the flames considerably but the room began filling with so much smoke everyone had no choice but to clear out.

Harley stubbornly continued to work to dismantle the burning wall, ignoring the others' warnings to get out. Thick smoke blinded him. He became overwhelmed and choked uncontrollably. His eyes burned and he fell to the floor.

He rolled onto his back and struggled to open his eyes. What he saw briefly before having to close them again was glowing yellow orange through a thick wall of black smoke. He had no idea which direction he was facing. He began to slide face down along the floor like a crocodile. Hoping to find his bearings, he felt table and chair legs and finally something very familiar—the piano. The piano was along the east wall opposite the door. He turned around and faced the other way and began to crawl again.

Outside the others were shouting into the burning saloon to try and guide Harley to safety. A man waved a lantern in the doorway in an attempt to provide a visual. Asa Helms ran inside. The smoke overtook him and he too dropped to the floor.

"Harley! Where are you? Follow my voice, son!" He heard the trapped man choking weakly from somewhere on the far side of the room. Suddenly, someone grabbed his legs and dragged him backwards. He wanted to stand but he was being pulled like a wheelbarrow. Splinters shot into the palms of his hands and he dropped onto his face. "What the hell? Who's there?"

He was dragged into the street and his legs dropped to the dirt. He rolled over in time to see Josh Adams run back into the saloon.

As many feared, the trench began overflowing. The channel designed to control any overflow had not been dug deeply enough. No one was really in danger of drowning and the water might help fight the fire, but it also might slow mobility when mobility and speed were imperative. People were now working almost knee deep in water and mud in some areas; and it was getting worse.

George thought quickly and grabbed three sticks of the remaining dynamite and bound them together. He got right in Felix's face. "Don't you hold out on me now, boy, let's go! Pops needs ya!" he said. He mounted the beast and kicked him hard in the haunches. Felix responded immediately and they raced for the channel. George lit the fuse and when they got close enough, he threw the tied sticks into the channel's center. George then yanked hard right on the bit and kicked Felix hard in haunches. The mule lunged once in the direction of town, and stopped cold! George kicked him again to no avail. "Wha—what're you doin'? C'mon, git, git! Gotta go! Gotta go!" George yelled at the animal as he jostled side to side in the saddle excitedly. "Move boy, move! Gonna blow up!" Felix stood, frozen. "Aw, geeze! C'mon!" George was getting ready to dismount and run for it when Felix bolted hard, back into town.

Behind them the loud blast threw droplets of water and mud a hundred feet into the air. George laughed loudly in triumph. "Atta boy! Good boy!" he hollered. Immediately the overflowing trench and channel receded, just enough to stop any potential flooding.

It was almost six in the morning. The wind began to howl and it was cold. The fire had raged nearly all night. Through the smoke everyone could see the gray clouds roll in overhead as heavy rain started to fall. The wind shifted North and the fire began to move steadily away from the town. It would be a long time before the fire was out, but for now, Tahosa was out of danger.

Everyone was beyond exhausted. Ely, Father Kettling and George looked around at what was left of their town. Somehow, most of the settlement had been spared. Asa's cabin had not been touched.

Five buildings in all were lost, including Holy Trinity and the saloon. The trading post had ignited but sustained minimal damage. It was a small building and was closest to the river so it was easy to contain.

Hopefully, the heavy rain would continue. Everyone knew, however that they would now be in danger of landslides and worked to barricade the settlement. The trench and the channel would remain.

The injured had been moved inside several homes and buildings, including Amy Peckman's restaurant. In all, forty nine had been hurt. Most were minor injuries, burns, cuts, etc. At least seventeen had died. Most of them were the Indians who had gotten trapped in the initial blaze. Nobody knew how many were unaccounted for.

Amy Peckman had started to cook what she could muster to start getting people fed. She poured some coffee for Josh Adams who was sitting up and talking a mile a minute. Harley McGuire lay nearby still sleeping. He had passed out on the saloon floor during the fire when Josh had rescued him.

After pulling Asa out of the burning saloon, Josh ran back into the fire blindly. He might not have found Harley if he hadn't tripped over the unconscious man and landed hard on his own face. He dragged Harley out by the arm, saving his life.

Eva walked in and sat down next to him. "Morning Mrs. Peckman", she said.

"Oh, Eva, darlin' it's so, so good to see you" Amy replied as she leaned down and hugged the girl. "How's your pa?"

"He's fine" she said, looking at Josh then back at Amy. "He was coughing for a while, but he's okay. He burned his arm kind o' bad but Father K. cleaned it up and wrapped it good. I'm so sorry about Mr. Peckman. He was a nice man".

Amy nodded almost tearing up. "Yes, he was", she said.

Josh said nothing. He looked down at his hands, fiddling with his knife.

Eva turned her attention back to Josh. "You saved my daddy's life, Josh Adams" Her lip quivered. "I thank you for that".

"Your pa 'd been fine without me. Harley's m' friend" he replied without looking up.

"He'd a gotten lost in there just like Harley if you hadn't done nuthin'. They'd both be dead and you know it"

"Well, uh,… Naw" he said sheepishly.

She leaned over and looked into his eyes. He lifted his head and looked back at her. In spite of the wool cap on her head and the dirt on her face she was still the most beautiful sight he'd ever laid eyes on.

"Don't you be modest Josh Adams. You saved two lives."

She kissed him on his lips and she turned and walked out of the restaurant. He turned bright red and watched her leave.

"Well, look at you, Mister. You're a hero, you know" said Amy.

"Nah,….maybe" Josh replied as he saw Eva run down the street. Then he smiled like he never smiled before.

Most of the tents in the miners' camp had been destroyed. Some of the miners began building temporary shelters to stay in until replacements could be made available.

Stewart Marcks was going to continue to sell liquor out of his home and put some of it on consignment in the trading post where George and Father Kettling would stay for the time being.

Stewart scolded them gruffly. "If I find out any of my rot gut is missing I'll beat both yer asses with a mule whip, priest or no priest!" All three men laughed.

"Well then, Stew let me be the first to buy a bottle" Fr. K said. They sat inside talking and drinking. For the first time in over a week they felt some sense of peace and quiet.

TWENTY SIX

MONDAY, SEPTEMBER 14TH, 1882.

HARLEY SLEPT THAT night in the store room of the restaurant. He woke up early and started coffee. It was sunup and he was feeling better but the smoke from the fire had taken its toll. He felt like he weighed a ton. In time his lungs would heal and so would the burns on his hands. He didn't remember being rescued.

While his friend, Josh snored in the corner on the floor under a table in the dining room, Harley poured himself a cup and walked from the kitchen into the dining area. The front door was open and the package lay on the porch. It was the typical brown wrapping tied with a purple ribbon. He took a double take and looked over at Josh who was now sitting up, staring at it.

Josh shot up and ran through the back room into the apartment area. He knocked loudly on Amy's door and when she answered she looked completely exhausted. She'd obviously been crying and still wore the same clothes from the day before, dusty and smeared with mud, blood and ash. It didn't appear she'd slept. She also seemed a little drunk.

"Mrs. Peckman, I…. Uh, you'd better come with me" he said.

Amy followed him out to the front room and stared down at the package. Her eyes blazed with hatred. The two men stood silently watching her. She leaned down and picked it up. It was heavy, soft in her hands. The paper crumpled.

Without hesitation, she angrily ripped it open, releasing a thick cloud of heavy dust and a flattened .44 caliber rifle slug which thudded to the floor. The note followed, drifting like a leaf to the wooden planks at her feet. She picked it up and read it silently:

> Ashes to ashes.
> Guns to rust,
> Gunplay is over,
> Incinerated to dust.
> Now he burns in Hell.

Amy looked down and fell to her knees. She scooped up some of her husband's ashes and examined them. Her eyes grew wide and she screamed in horror.

TWENTY SEVEN

L ATER, FATHER KETTLING and a number of other men dug several shallow graves in the cemetery for those lost in the fire. One was for Ed Peckman, whose remains had been so cruelly delivered to his widow that morning.

He and Ely offered space in the cemetery to the Indians who had lost loved ones. A group of angry white men objected. A very cranky Father K. quickly addressed the situation with harsh words. "We are all God's damned children you sons o' bitches and these Redskins are gonna lie side by side with me and yourn! Like it or not, they fought that fire too!"

Ely and several of his deputies then handed shovels to the protesters and ordered them to start digging. They refused, throwing the shovels to the ground. The small group of five Indians that were present stepped forward and picked them up. One of them said "We will bury our own. We need no help from them".

Ely addressed the protesters. "We don't have time for this kind of horseshit, boys. Hell's in town and we're *all* in this. You'll show respect and work together or you'll leave. I'll see to it m'self. We don't need no burden from the likes of you".

Throughout most of the day, many in town continued to labor at constructing a defensive wall to route potential landslides. A barrier had been made of six foot high, thickly stacked logs a few yards east of the moat. It was aimed at the facing mountain like a giant arrow head. Hopefully, it would deflect any oncoming debris to either side of town, minimizing any threat. It had been reinforced with rock, support beams and anything else that might work: furniture, wagons, plows, etc.

All anyone could do now was wait.

Before sundown, two walls of thick mud broke from the charred mountain above. The first sped down the trail toward the miners' camp. The other crashed down the mountainside directly above, snapping and uprooting charred trees under its dense weight. Some ran for the high ground to the east. Others took cover behind the large barrier.

Kevin Marcks could see the avalanche coming fast from where he stood behind the wall. "I gotta find a new place to live" he said to a man next to him. They both nodded.

The first slide easily covered what was left of the miners' camp and continued harmlessly into the river and channel. The second slide, much bigger in size crashed into the barrier with earth shaking force. In some places logs were knocked loose and toppled onto the people inside. Mud flowed over the top but most of it was held back and flowed along the sides of the pointed structure. The moat had helped slow the mud but the barrier was being pummeled by earth and debris. Nonetheless, it held strong, for the most part.

During the assault, one thick, heavy log shot like a javelin over the barrier, directly onto a crouching George Mcquirving. The crunch of his bones could be heard by everyone around him. He became pinned, face down in the muck. Mud flowed over the wall, completely burying him. People rushed and desperately tried to dig him out. Two other logs rolled from the top of the barrier and rolled away. After what seemed like an eternity, the slide began to lose momentum and settle. The barrier had mostly held. The town was safe, but people continued to work frantically to uncover George and others. The log on top of George was cemented in the mud making it impossible to move. He would suffocate to death if it wasn't lifted.

George was conscious but he knew he was going to die. He was completely paralyzed and unable to breathe. Nonetheless, he felt no pain and experienced an indescribable peace. He had no ability to move. There was only darkness.

When the light came, he saw long gone family and friends reaching out to welcome him. Millie Orman was there too. Her smile was more beautiful than he had remembered. He looked down and watched as the town worked to help him and the others before joining those in the radiant and welcoming light.

TWENTY EIGHT

T HE MONK WATCHED from high atop the mountain. The mere weight of his oxen and wagon had been enough to send the wall of earth in its destructive path. The stupid miner had started the fire but it was he, the terrible monk who had sent the avalanche. It was the delicious combination of good and evil which had crippled the town so horribly.

The killer would continue his part of the job he had felt so compelled to complete- *to annihilate this putrid, holy parish....* *Tahosa.*

TWENTY NINE

WHEN THEY FINALLY recovered George's body, Father Kettling knelt beside his best friend and prayed. After, he somberly walked back to where his church had stood and sat down and cried. A faint breeze blew his hair and he looked around. He seemed to feel George's spirit was there with him.

He thought about the tragedies that had transpired in just over one week. He found it completely incomprehensible. It was clear to even the most atheist of men that there was clearly something at work here which was not of this world.

He needed to do research. He was hundreds of miles from Denver where the Archdiocese was located. That's also where the best library was. Boulder was the closest major town but he had no way of knowing whether or not it would be worth it to travel that far if he couldn't find what he needed.

He decided to write to the Denver Archdiocese and the Vatican itself. He never necessarily believed in demons of Biblical proportions but something needed to be done.

THIRTY

FOR SOME, ENOUGH was enough. In the days following the disaster a number of settlers and their families left Tahosa, never to return. There was a serial killer on the loose and half the town was destroyed.

Jakob Mueller arrived in town late that morning. He had missed his son's funeral. Travel had been delayed due to the fire.

Before he left Denver, he and the governor had made arrangements for medical supplies, food, and building materials to be delivered by wagon train to the small mining town. Tents would be erected to serve as a church, hospital, a saloon, public housing and storage for foodstuffs.

The town and work in the mine resumed. The barrier and the moat would remain as precaution against the still lingering possibility of more slides.

As weeks went by there were no signs of the weird monk. Occasionally, a search party would deploy but would always return without news. Many began to think that he had eventually died of his bullet wounds or had perished in the fire. Father K. was not convinced, however. His letters to the Denver Archdiocese and the Vatican explained what had transpired in the little town in detail. They had corresponded accordingly and the Pope responded by stating he was considering sending a party to investigate.

The Rocky Mountain News had published several articles on the events and a few national newspapers were also beginning to print stories about the occurrences.

Nobody knew anything of the weird monk with the purple wagon. He had never been seen nor heard of until the reign of terror began. Some had claimed to have seen him in the days and weeks following the fire but most claims were considered fabricated.

Father Kettling was sent books and articles on demonology and the occult by the Vatican and various Archdioceses around the country. He studied as much as possible and continued his correspondences in the weeks to come.

PART III

THIRTY ONE

Friday, October 29, 1882.

For Asa Helms, the harvest was over. Much of his crop had had been burned in the fire the previous month. Eva would continue to work part time in the trading post every day until planting began the next spring.

He'd lost a considerable amount of money this year but was able to cover some of his losses by serving as deputy sheriff. Seeing as much of the town's food and supplies were still being stored in tents, more security was needed. It was early evening and he was on duty.

In the past few weeks his daughter had taken an inexplicable interest in Josh and in spite of the fact that Josh had recently turned twenty years old and had finally grown up (sort of), Asa still didn't particularly like her keeping company with him. He was also definitely not pleased that she was showing interest in a white man.

Tonight she was supposed to bring him dinner and she was late....again. She and Josh were undoubtedly somewhere doing God knows what. He didn't like to think about it.

Eva and Josh were in the Helms' cabin. She was beneath him and gripped him tightly as he made love to her. She shuddered and moaned softly. After, they both breathed heavily. She smiled and kissed him.

She glanced at the clock. She was supposed to deliver supper to her father forty five minutes ago.

"Shit!" she said as she jumped out of bed and started to dress. Josh laughed and said, "You in trouble, little girl!"

"Shut up", she said laughing. "This is your fault".

She gathered some beans, an ear of corn and a thick slice of roast beef and packed it for her father. "Do I look alright?" she asked Josh.

"Hell yeah, you look alright".

"Good. Gotta go, Josh. Don't want nobody seein' you hangin' around here. Go on, git!".

"Hell. You comin' back?"

"Gonna have dinner with m'daddy". "Alright. I love you, Eva."

"I love you too Josh Adams. Can't believe I'm sayin' it, but I do."

"Still think I'm a little boy with a little pecker?"She started laughing. "Nah. Now you just a big pecker".Josh smiled and kissed her before he finished dressing and ran out the back door.

THIRTY TWO

E LY AND FR. Kettling sat up late that night in the new tent saloon drinking. Stewart was tending bar. The priest was re-reading the letter he'd received two days ago from the Vatican. A cold wind blew and the wood burning stove heated the room nicely.

The priest wasn't sure if demons or other entities could take human form or not, or what they were really capable of. He'd put in countless hours of research over the last weeks on the subject. There were so many different devils, angels, demons and such that he knew he'd never be able to study all of them. Sure, there was Baal, one of the seven princes of Hell, Beelzebub, Lucifer or Satan, etc. but most of what he'd read seemed like nothing more that lore. Most of the names he'd never even heard of. How in the world could he narrow any one or more of them down? On the other hand, he noted that the pattern of recent events in Tahosa *did* match certain historical accounts of demonic activity throughout world history. He had implored the Holy Church to look into it and felt he had the beginnings of a pretty strong case for investigation and help. Nonetheless, the letter stated that the Vatican would not be sending anyone. Instead, a team from the Denver Archdiocese was asked to travel to the town to "inquire thoroughly" whatever that meant. He thought that surely he'd made enough of a case for formal investigation. He complained to Stewart and Ely about the situation.

"Paul, you know I ain't much of a church type" said Stewart. "You really think demons and 'spookys' can attack people?"

"Stew, I do and they did. You can't tell me that stuff that happened was just bad luck. Before now I wouldn't have said they could either. I always thought there's the devil, demons and whatnot. I mean, I never saw possession or anything like that in my years but you can't deny what happened here. It ain't normal".

"Well, no, it ain't" replied Stew. "I think the worst is over, though. Ain't nobody seen nor heard nuthin' about that killer monk in some time. I bet he's dead. From what George said they filled him up pretty good with lead... and then the fire, you know?"

"I'm not so sure. I get a feelin' we ain't heard or seen the last of that damned wagon driver".

Asa was dozing off in a chair outside the grain & food stores tent. It was late and Harley McGuire would be along soon to take the overnight guard. He stood up to wake himself up a little bit and shake off the cold. Thunder rumbled in the distance. "Little clear for thunder", he said to himself and looked up at a clear, starry sky. He walked around the side of the tent in time to see two faint lights far up the western slope of the mountain moving between the trees. Some folks had said they'd seen these on a couple of occasions but no one really made too much out of it. They were so distant that they were barely visible. They may have been reflections from the wet ground. Some of the Indians associated them with a local legend of lost lovers. Some even believed they were ghosts of those who died in the fire. Asa watched them for several minutes before they finally faded away. He turned to walk back to the entrance of the tent and walked right into Harley who, without knowing had been standing behind him the entire time.

"Gaahh, ah! Dammit all, man! What the hell you doin'?" yelled Asa.

"What the hell *you* doin', Asa?"asked an irritated Harley.

"Damn, don't sneak up on folks like that".

"I was just watchin' what you was watchin'".

"You saw it?"

"Yeah, I saw it. Was standin' right here. Lights movin' around up there. Who you think it is?"

"I don't know, but I don't like it. I'm goin' t' find Ely. See you tomorrow"

The wind began to blow fiercely. Asa walked to the trading post and knocked on the door. Ely did not answer. He tried to open the door but it was locked. He walked to the tent saloon and found Ely, Fr. K. and Stewart sharing a bottle of whiskey.

"Evenin, Asa" said Ely.

"Father, Ely, Stew. Uh, hey, Harley and I saw some lights moving around 'bout halfway up the mountain there and....".

"You did!" Father K interrupted excitedly. He jumped to his feet and ran out into the wind. He looked up to the mountain and saw nothing.

"They gone now" Asa said.

"What'd they look like? How long were they there?" asked the priest.

"Looked like somebody was walkin' around up there with lanterns—two or three. Maybe for a couple o' minutes. They kind of a pale purple color. That's why I came to find you. Don't like it at all".

"What do you think, Paul?" asked Ely.

"I don't know. I got no idea. I've seen 'em too once or twice but didn't want to say anything. Folks 'round here are jumpy enough. Last thing I wanna do is get people all worked up again"

Half a mile up the hill, the monk stood in a corner of the cemetery. His hood was not pulled over his head. He held a lantern at his side. It glowed a dim, bluish purple. His face looked as if it had been frozen in the middle of an insane, maniacal laugh. His eyes were wide. A thin trace of spittle lined his pale, blue lips as the wind whipped around him, his robes flapping.

He stood about 5'6". His hair was short, curly dark blond. He was deathly pale and his fat, unshaven face reflected the bluish light.

He had rested and the time to return had come.

THIRTY THREE

JAKOB MUELLER HAD reorganized the mine's management and was running over some loose ends with his younger son, Erick who would take over as chief foreman. It was early and men were arriving to work when one of his employees burst into his office. "Mr. Mueller! We found somethin'. You'd better come quick!" The men hurried to the lift outside.

They climbed in and were lowered nearly one hundred feet to the tunnel floor. They briskly walked the quarter of a mile to the end and stopped where a crowd of others were standing. Jakob elbowed his way through and stood in silent shock at the horrific scene before him.

The head of Dr. Del Stigg, who'd been missing for weeks hung from the ceiling like a lantern. Actually, he *was* a lantern. The inside of his skull had been hollowed out and a chain had been bolted to the top of his head. A fixed candle flickered behind his empty eye sockets.

The blasting face in the rock wall behind him had been drilled the day before. The drill holes now oozed with gore. It appeared that the rest of Dr. Stigg had been stuffed into them.

Jakob was a man who was able to compose himself and respond quickly and effectively. He had proven this as a field artillery officer during the Franco Prussian War twelve years prior. He turned and faced his men. "Alright" he began. "Clear zee shaft und fetch Mr. Vhitaker und his deputies. Erick, zee men will continue der verk elsvhere in de mine. Come".

He walked back to the lift and the others followed. Two men were ordered to stay at the scene until Ely arrived.

"Well, he's creative, I'll give him that" Ely said as he peered into the yellow-orange glowing eyes of Del Stigg's head. He swallowed hard and wiped the cold sweat from his forehead. He felt sick to his stomach and a little bit dizzy. "Why now? Where the hell's he been all this time?"

"Maybe he was right here under our noses" Erick commented. "It's a mine, after all. There are sections of this place that even I haven't seen".

"True" said Jakob. "Mr. Vhitaker, please allow de men to continue verking in zee ozzer sections of de mine today. You may investigate, but too much has been lost to close for de day. I recommend blasting dis face to clean and burn the rest of Dr. Stigg's remains. It vill be too difficult to try and pull zee body from zese holes".

Ely now looked completely ill. He and the others grimaced as they looked at the dripping holes in the wall. "Alright" he said. "Take the head down and cover it up. Take him directly to Father Kettling. He'll make arrangements. As for the rest of it, uh...." He shrugged. "Blow it up".

A carriage carrying two men arrived at the trading post later that morning. Driving was a young priest named Father

Dennis. His passenger was Monsignor Clemente. Both were from Sacred Heart Parish in

Denver, the men the Denver Archdiocese had sent.

Eva gave directions to the church. "It's down a block and on the right. Can't miss it. Father K is gonna be so glad you're here. Lots o' bad stuff happenin'" she said. "Folks say there was another man killed just this mornin'. In a awful way too".

They thanked her and drove to meet Fr. Kettling.

Father K had made a sign for his new church which read Holy Trinity Catholic Mission. He was standing on a chair hanging it above the entrance when his guests arrived.

"Holy horse shit, am I glad to see you men!" he gruffed as he stepped down.

"Father, please!" said Father Dennis.

"Of course, excuse me, gentlemen. I'm Paul Kettling, nice to meet you."

"We understand, Father. It seems you've had some major problems here" replied the Monsignor. "I'm Monsignor Clemente from Sacred Heart Parish and this is Father Dennis, my assistant".

Surveying the layout of the town from where they stood, Father Dennis spoke. "It looks like a fortress here".

"Well, I suppose it is, more or less" replied Fr. K. "Come on in and I'll tell you everything".

The three men went inside where they said a brief prayer and settled at the table near the altar. Their host poured three glasses of whiskey. Fr. K told the story from the beginning. He told them how Millie was found, the death of the foreman at the mine, the fire, everything. He also told them that he'd heard the town doctor had been found mutilated that morning.

An hour and a half later, Harley McGuire rode to the church. He dismounted and walked briskly inside carrying the box containing Dr. Stigg's hollowed head.

"Father, um, excuse me".

"Harley, come in. This is Monsignor Clemente and Father Dennis from Sacred Heart in Denver. The Archdiocese sent them here to look into this whole mess" Fr. K said as they stood.

"Pleased to meet you gentlemen" replied Harley as he handed the box to Fr. K. The priest held the box. It was light in his hands. "What is this?" he asked.

"Uh, you all better sit down" Harley said as he swallowed thickly.

The monsignor and Fr. Dennis did not like the uncertain, frightened look on his face. They looked at each other, then back at him and slowly sat down. Fr. K. opened the lid of the box and peered inside. He began breathing rapidly and stumbled backwards, dropping the box on the table. Harley caught him before he fell. The other two clergymen looked inside the container. The monsignor's jaw clenched as he stared, wide eyed at the contents. He reached in and lifted the head out and held it up. Father Dennis stared in shock and fell back into his chair.

That night the two priests and the monsignor dined with Ely in Amy's restaurant. None of them had much of an appetite after what they'd seen. They found it more palatable to order a bottle of whiskey from Marck's place. Kevin Marcks delivered it and Fr. K. gave him a generous tip.

"They said that the rest of him was packed into blasting holes. They couldn't get him out so they blasted the face to try and incinerate the remains" said Fr. Kettling. Amy overheard, covered her mouth and ran into the kitchen. Fr. Dennis stood and went after her when Fr. K. grabbed his arm and spoke. "Don't go after her, son. She just lost her husband in a way that was just about as bad. Best let her be". Father Dennis nodded and sat back down.

"I've been reading up on materials sent from Denver and Rome" Fr. K continued. "At first it felt like maybe I was reading too much into what's been happening here, but under the circumstances I don't know how else to address this".

"After everything you've told us here and in your letters we're familiar with the situation. So is the Pontiff" said the Monsignor. Somewhat surprised, Father Kettling raised his eyebrows. "Rome does not want to send a team here until we report our findings in detail. I'm sure if these horrible things keep happening, a team may be dispatched".

"I took the liberty of taking Dr. Stigg's remains to the undertaker, Father" said Fr. Dennis. "He said to stop by in the morning for instructions on how to proceed".

"Thank you. Much obliged".

In the restaurant they poured over the research materials. Fr. K had apologized to Amy for what he'd blurted out earlier. "Oh, Paul, that's not your fault. I would've heard it one way or another. Horrible, just horrible" she'd replied. The men paid her and walked back to the church where they would continue researching the unexplained, Satanism and demonology.

By midnight the men were ready to retire for the evening. Out of all of their research, one entity stood out to them. He was known throughout history by different names and in different cultures. Ancient Hebrew defined his name, *Abaddon* to mean 'destruction'. The Book of Revelations explains he is a fallen angel, "King of the Demons of Hell". He commands an army of locusts set on destroying man. Greek text refers to him as Apollyon.

"Gentlemen, I feel we really might be trying to see too much into this" Monsignor Clemente announced as he closed the book he'd been examining. "Although we must be prepared for the worst and in spite of all of the strange eyewitness testimonies and goings on, this still looks to be the work of an elusive serial killer".

"He's not just a serial killer, Monsignor," said Fr. K. "The repeated, horrifying events that have taken place here in just weeks surpass anything any normal man is capable of. Look at our town, for God's sake, or even what's left of it! What's more, that wagon he drives is the biggest anybody's ever seen.

What the hell is it for? The whole thing just emanates evil. Ask anybody. It's size is….how it can even move down this little town block let alone through complete forests where the trails are barely big enough for a buggy to pass through is beyond me. I hope you see that wagon, Monsignor so you see what it is we're dealing with. Then tell me if you think he's just a serial killer. He was atop that south plateau. It's not possible to even get up there with a wagon. Only narrow hunting trails lead up there. Yet, there he was the morning of Millie Orman's funeral. The whole town saw him. He disappeared before anybody even got to him on horseback. It's impossible. Im-poss-ible! Now folks are seein' those lights up there moving around all over the place. Yep, got more than just a killer on our hands, sir!"

Monsignor Clemente would not have to wait long before he saw the wagon for himself.

THIRTY FOUR

EVA CLOSED UP the trading post for the night, locked the door and started walking alone back to her cabin. It was quiet and a soft breeze cooled the night. The stars shone brightly overhead.

Coyotes that used to be heard howling in the distance were rarely heard these days. The hoots of owls had ceased all together weeks ago.

She came to the end of the block and passed the church. She looked up the road leading to the cemetery. She knew she had no business at this time of night walking that half mile to Tahosa City Cemetery, yet something was drawing her there.

She carried a .44 caliber Peacemaker that Ely had kept under the trading post counter for protection. He advised she carry it home at night herself as long as she wouldn't forget to bring it back the next morning, of course.

She took the gun out of the holster and held it in front of her with both hands and started up the road to the cemetery. Everything seemed to become even quieter. She could see the faint glow of purple light ahead.

Halfway up the road, the light emanating from the cemetery revealed the path and its surroundings. Occasionally she turned around, the gun extended. She knew how to defend herself if need be. Ahead she heard the huffs of restless animals.

She figured it was probably nothing more than stray cattle that had wandered up this way which happened from time to time.

As she approached the cemetery gates, she saw a figure standing there. Soft purple light glowed beside him. She almost turned and ran but felt the overwhelming urge to approach. She walked forward to within thirty feet of him and stopped.

"Hello?" She said. No answer. "I said hello!" Still no response. She moved closer and slowed her pace, readying herself for anything. The figure didn't move.

On the other side of the yard she saw the oxen and the giant wagon partially covered by foliage. She knew immediately who it was. Terror gripped her.

"You stay right there!" she yelled. "You stay right where you are! My daddy's a deputy sheriff and you gonna be under arrest". The monk said nothing. She really had no idea what to do. She had never been this frightened in her life but shooting him down didn't seem exactly like an appealing solution. Nonetheless, that's exactly what she knew she had to do.

"Don't move!" she said again with a shaky voice. She glanced to either side of the monk. Her eyes widened. The glowing light basked several graves in a soft, purplish hue and she looked back at the monk. She closed her eyes and fired twice. The gun thundered, recoiling violently. She opened her eyes and fired again. She had missed all three times.

Behind him from the direction of the wagon, a swirling tornado of black rose from the trees and spiraled toward her. Their forms were not clearly visible but there seemed to be a million of them. *Birds?* she thought. As they came closer she could make out the webbed wings of thousands of bats. They squeaked and flapped angrily as they came at her. The purple light reflected off of them.

She let out a blood curdling scream and turned and sprinted hard back down the road. Flapping wings and tiny furry bodies crashed into her. Several became entangled in her hair. She tried desperately to escape and fell, hitting at them and rolling on the ground. She stood back up and ran again when dozens of hands suddenly came out of nowhere, grabbing her. She saw figures everywhere shadowed in the darkness. They pulled her to the ground and pinned her.

She screamed again in horror when the bats rose and spiraled away.

"Eva!" her father yelled. "Eva, honey, it's me! You're okay!" She looked at the people above her and followed her father's voice. "Daddy!" she screamed.

"It's okay, honey! We're here! We got you!"

Eva stared back at the faces looking down at her. She saw Ely, Fr. K, Kevin Marcks, her pa and several others. They'd heard the shots and her screams and wasted no time in reaching her. She'd made it almost half way down when they intercepted her. They too had seen the purple glow up from the cemetery.

She was taken down to her and her father's cabin where she was given a generous glass of whiskey and some water. Josh had heard the commotion and sat on the edge of her bed holding her hand. A few white men scowled at what they saw. Asa did too but his little girl had had the shit scared clean out of her and she needed her man, not just her daddy. He allowed it. It was time folks get used to it he guessed. He'd have to get used to it too.

THIRTY FIVE

AMY PECKMAN HAD made up a bed for Monsignor Clemente in Dr. Stiggs' old apartment. Father Dennis would sleep at the church in a cot set up by Fr. K. The Monsignor and Ely had returned to the restaurant and stayed up late talking.

Eva had told them about her experience. When a group of men including Ely and the three clergymen went to investigate they found nothing aside from a giant path of broken and splintered trees leading away from the rear of the cemetery. The path of destruction led one hundred feet into the woods where it inexplicably stopped.

Msgr. C finished his coffee and inquired about Ed Peckman's death. It was painful, but Amy obliged and told him about the horrific event.

"A lot of us saw him that first day in town" she said referring to the monk. "Ed got run over by that wagon he drives. Apparently, both oxen had trampled him and then the wheels crushed him. One of the miners, George McQuirving was with him and said the rig 'moved like lightning'. He probably never felt a thing, thank God. Wasn't nuthin' left".

The Monsignor shivered and shook his head saying, "Dear God, I'm so sorry".

"Thank you, Monsignor. You sure you want to stay in Del's place? I mean, after what happened to him and the time I saw that crazy monk back there, I think twice about going inside my own place".

"Don't you worry about me" he replied. "I'll be just fine and thank you so much again for the accommodations, Mrs. Peckman".

"It'll be nice having a man around again. I really don't like staying alone here" she replied.

She smiled, said good night and retired.

THIRTY SIX

SUNDAY MORNING, ALL HALLOW'S EVE, 1882.

MSGR. CLEMENTE, FATHER Kettling and Father Dennis said Mass together for a crowded tent in honor of the Feast of All Saints. It was sunny out and unseasonably warm. Dr. Del Stigg's mostly absent remains would be buried in the cemetery the following day.

After Mass, Eva again helped Amy in the restaurant. Asa helped clear a few tables himself after eating a quick lunch with Ely. Folks enjoyed the weather by going hunting or fishing, strolling around town, picnicking, etc.

Ely went home after lunch to retrieve his fishing gear and he and Msgr. Clemente walked east about three quarters of a mile down river. They dropped their lines in Ely's favorite spot and he pulled out a flask and offered it to the Monsignor. "No thanks, Ely. It's a holiday, after all. Just a rule of mine".

"Alright. Well, Cheers to all the saints then" replied Ely as he took a long pull. The Monsignor laughed.

"Cheers indeed!"

Fishing was excellent that day and the men decided they would host a trout and salmon dinner at the church that night for Fr. K, Fr. Dennis and Amy. As time went on, Msgr. Clemente decided that even though it was a holiday, one or two nips from Ely's flask wouldn't make any difference. He was having a good time. Aside from the horror that he had heard and seen he found the people here extremely strong willed. He'd heard that a number of the population had left due to the circumstances but those that remained were hard working, helpful and friendly.

Suddenly, Ely felt the hair stand up on the back of his neck as he stood and stared across the river. He could sense the presence.

"You alright, Ely?" asked Msgr. Clemente.

"He's here. I can tell" Ely replied, nervously grinding his teeth.

Over the rushing water they didn't immediately hear the sound of cracking and splintering trees coming from across the river, but could see that something colossal and destructive was moving among them. A cold wind hit the men as the rig slowly emerged from the forest and stopped to face them.

Msgr. Clemente could not believe the size of the two huge oxen as they stood motionless. Behind them, the enormous wagon, dark purple in color loomed as much as twenty feet in height. The Monsignor's mouth gaped open. He dropped his fishing pole and the rapids immediately swept it downstream.

Ely grabbed his shotgun and waded almost waist deep into the rapids. He aimed and fired once, then again. The canvas of the wagon shook behind the hooded monk as he jerked. The second shot clearly hit him in the chest. The dust flew from his robe as the impact threw him backwards. Ely reloaded and managed another shot when he tripped and fell forward, smashing his knee on a jagged rock. The gun fell, sinking.

The monk sat back up, cocked his head to the side and calmly watched what happened next.

Ely rolled sideways into the rushing water and tried to correct himself. The current pulled him farther out. The pain in his knee was terrible. He cried out and tried to stand but the water quickly and without warning sucked him into the raging rapids. The Monsignor jumped into the river to help his friend. Now chest deep in the current, he realized he too would be taken away by the rushing water if he did not retreat. He extended Ely's fishing rod in an attempt to help but it was futile. Ely never even saw it.

The violent water pulled Ely into the icy maelstrom and shot him downriver. The first boulder hit him in the chest and he was pulled under. The shock took his breath and he gasped for air, inhaling only liquid. The current then shot him forward, hitting his shoulder on a second rock, breaking his upper left arm. The pain was excruciating.

The rapids carried him down river at an accelerating speed. He tried in vain to protect himself from the relentless blows as he was pulled under again and again. The intense pressure sucked him underwater one last time, lodging him between two boulders. Within moments the intense force of the water shot him out and upward like a champagne cork. He landed, his face smashing onto a granite slab. He was knocked unconscious immediately, if not killed. Blood poured from his nose and mouth as he was taken down river.

Msgr. Clemente watched his new friend tumble like a rag doll down the rapids. He knew that if Ely survived it would be a miracle. The Monsignor tried to keep up with him as he ran along the bank and find a way to help but there was nothing he could do. He turned and looked back in the direction of the wagon in time to see it slowly roll away back into the tree line.

The Monsignor realized it was senseless to run farther down river and ran back to town as fast as he could. Out of breath and on the verge of panic he reached the restaurant and told Amy what had happened. Amy ran into the saloon and a group of men including Harley and Asa immediately mounted up and headed for the river. Eva watched as they galloped away past the trading post.

When the dust cleared she saw something on the trading post door's small window and walked over to see what it was. From a distance it looked like a smudge but when she got close enough to see it, she put her hands over her mouth and gasped. A small, upside down cross had been painted in blood on the pane.

Amy, the Monsignor, Josh and a crowd of others gathered around to witness the ugly mark. Eva went inside with Josh. There was a package sitting on the counter. Eva just stared at it as Josh picked it up, looking at Eva as if to ask whether or not he should unwrap the disturbing gift.

"Don't open it" she said, clearly shaken.

"I won't if you don't want me to" he replied. "We should give it to your pa, though". She nodded and they stepped back outside.

Everyone looked at the package with the purple ribbon in Josh's hands. Msgr. Clemente addressed the small crowd. "For weeks I've read the letters from Father Kettling. For weeks I found much of what he said to be extraordinary and fantastic. I have not been here for even two full days, yet what I have seen I find peculiar, horrifying and inexplicably dangerous. I shall write to Rome immediately. Something must be done".

MONDAY, NOVEMBER 1, 1882.

Eva opened the trading post for business as usual. The sun had just come up and it was a clear, cool morning. She had been up

all night worrying about Ely. She was weary and it was difficult to concentrate on her duties. It was safe to say that at the
very least he was terribly injured. The man had been so nice
to her and her father all of these years. She loved him like a
grandfather. She also knew that the town's greatest leader
was now missing, possibly dead. Her father and the other men
who'd gone to search for him found nothing. Another team had
already left this morning to continue the search. What would
she do without him?

Later, at about nine o'clock a.m., two Indians arrived in a
cart. Eva was sweeping the floor when she saw them and went
outside to assist. They seemed like regular customers passing
through town to refresh and buy supplies.

"Mornin'" she said. "What can I get for you?"

"Morning ma'am" one of the Indians replied as he turned
and looked in the back of the cart. "We won't be needing anything".

Scowling, she walked to the back of the cart and looked
inside. There lay the body, wrapped in a wool blanket. It was
him. She gripped the side of the wagon. "No!" she cried as
she rocked back and forth, tears starting to stream down her
cheeks. "No!" People heard and ran to her. They saw the body
and gathered around.

Amy saw and heard the commotion and ran to the trading
post herself. "Oh, no!" she said quietly as she approached the
small cart. She covered her mouth and began to cry softly. "God
have mercy! Oh no!" She went directly to Eva who was now
crying loudly. Amy could only do her best to comfort the girl.

Very early that morning members of the Arapahoe
Indian tribe six miles to the southeast discovered Ely's body.
He'd been almost unrecognizable had it not been for the watch

in his pocket where his name was engraved. Children fetching water found him floating face down in a calm, inlet pool.

These people knew Ely. They were customers of his from time to time and he'd always been good to them. They cleaned him up, wrapped him in a blanket, lifted him into the cart and took him home to Tahosa.

Father Dennis climbed into the cart, knelt beside the body and prayed. Ely was then taken to the undertaker's office where Father Kettling waited. Fr. K had arrived earlier to retrieve Del Stigg for his funeral. He would hold two funerals this week.

It seemed the monk may be starting to make up for lost time.

THIRTY SEVEN

D R. DEL STIGG was laid to rest that afternoon. The coffin containing his remains was lowered into the grave as a large crowd sang Amazing Grace. Dr. Stigg had been a very devout Catholic and frequently traveled to other settlements, offering his services free of charge to those who could not afford them.

When Influenza had gripped a Ute settlement three years ago he set up a medical station outside the camp. He and others provided treatment for the sick as best as they could. Two children and one elderly man had died from the sickness. Had he not been there, many more might have perished. Many of the people from that community attended his burial.

As Father Kettling read his final reading, his mind wandered. He thought of the horrific way Del had been found and now another of his friends, Ely was dead, battered beyond belief. He trailed off mid-sentence and stared down at the pine coffin in silence. He became overwhelmed with grief.

The attendees at the funeral lifted their heads and looked at him. "Father?" said Msgr. Clemente. "Would you like me to continue?" Fr. K cleared his throat and shook his head.

"No, Monsignor, thank you. I'll continue".

With that, he concluded his reading as tears poured down his cheeks and his voice wavered. When he was finished, the crowd crossed themselves and turned to head back toward town.

Father Kettling fell to his knees and broke down and cried. Monsignor Clemente stood next to him in silence and squeezed his new friend's shoulder. It was all he could do.

After the service, Eva and Josh went to the trading post and sat at the table outside talking. Asa returned to his cabin.

Asa picked up the package which had been left in the trading post the day before. His hands shook as he held it. It was light like the others. "What if I just didn't open the damn thing?" He asked himself aloud. He considered burning it outside but feared the consequences. Nobody knew exactly what they were dealing with, but at this point everyone was certain that it was from Hell.

He took a deep breath, untied the ribbon and tore open the brown paper. He held the contents and examined it. It was a box like what had been found at Millie Orman's. He was breathing heavily. Sweat was forming on his brow. What if this was a curse directed at his little girl? He had to know.

Quickly, he opened the box and looked inside. There was the note like always. He held it up and read it. It said:

> The magistrate's blood,
> Marks the door,
> Where once was seen,
> Is seen no more.
> Thy blood fuels....

Asa exhaled loudly. The poem made no mention of his daughter and he felt relieved... for now. He pulled out the remaining contents of the box. Tied with a small white ribbon, a standard purple hanker chief contained something small and heavy. He untied it and shotgun pellets spilled everywhere. He remembered how Amy opened the package in her restaurant and a bullet had fallen out. These must be the shot from Ely's .12 gauge. Could the monk be shot but not killed?

The purple hanker chief was embroidered with the letters E.W. He thought about his friend and all he had done in welcoming him and Eva; and helping them get established in the little town all those years ago. "It's time" he said out loud as he stood. "This ends now!" he shouted loudly to an empty room.

He picked up several of the shot pellets and took them along with the hanker chief and the poem to the church.

The three clergymen read the poem one by one, silently. Fr. Dennis looked at the Monsignor and nodded.

"We gotta do somethin'!" Asa said.

"Mr. Helms," said the Monsignor. "We all understand the gravity of this. Beit supernatural, evil, what have you, you are correct. It must be destroyed and with the Lord's help, hopefully we can find a way to do this. Please, sit down and let me show you something".

Asa sat at the table which was stacked with various letters and books. Fr. Dennis and Fr. K sat on either side of him. Msgr. Clemente continued. "Satan and his demons are documented throughout history in all cultures. They have been explained as the product of pure evil brought by Satan himself or even man. They come in many, many forms. They *can* be controlled. Some are fallen angels, some aren't. Together, Father's K, myself and Dennis have done extensive research for weeks. So have my associates in Rome, Denver and even Boulder. We finally feel we may have an idea of what we're dealing with here".

Fr. K. picked up one of the books, opened it to a marked page and handed it to Asa. "Now, this is going to sound pretty extraordinary, but hear us out" he said. "The bodies of Millie Orman and Johann Mueller showed little, almost no signs of blood when found, remember?" Asa nodded in confirmation. "Well, we think there's an explanation for this". Father Dennis continued. "Again, throughout history there have been stories of demons in all cultures who are blamed for death and destruction to mankind. For example, In Christianity, The Book of Revelations refers to a fallen angel named 'Abbadon'. In Greek text he's called 'Appollyon'. He is hell bent on hurting man. However, there is a more likely candidate we may be dealing with here. Its name is Karau, a demon who is known for causing death in the world. He affects people with tragedies & illness, famine, rape, murder, etc."

"Now, Mr. Helms" said the Monsignor. "If this is in fact the case, these are not the only entities we believe we're dealing with. We think that there may be more. In fact, we think your daughter encountered at least one of them". Asa tilted his head and stared wide eyed at what he was hearing.

"What the hell?" he said. "Are you serious?"

"Asa, I told you. Please bear with us. It sounds as crazy to us as it does to you but we need to look at the possibilities here no matter how absurd they seem" said Fr. K. "We have a man crashing through whole sections of thick forests on an impossibly huge rig with two very oversized oxen. We have mutilated bodies with no blood. We h—"

"We have something that Ely Whitaker pumped three rounds into then violently yanked him into that river without touching him" interrupted the Monsignor. "You hold that same shot in your hand, Mr. Helms. I tried to make sense of this by telling myself that Ely only fell, but that's not what happened. I saw it. He was pulled by something. What other explanations do you have, sir? Believe mewe'd love to explore other more acceptable possibilities".

Asa stood up from the table and bit his lip. He walked around the room deep in thought. Fr. K noticed how much the man's hair had grayed in just weeks. "More than one....uh, *demons*?" said Asa.

"Two, at least" Fr. Dennis replied.

"How'm I supposed to believe this?

"You don't have to, Mr. Helms. We're trying every approach here. We're not Pinkerton detectives and until we hear from Rome I feel that it's up to us to try anything we can. We have nothing to lose" said Msgr. Clemente.

"Two" Asa said again. He scratched the stubble on his chin and shook his head. "I don't know.... uh....What makes you think there's two?"

"Remember the bats that attacked Eva?" asked Fr. Dennis.

"Uh huh".

"That's a second one".

"He's best known as Jiliaya, if that's who he or it is. It moves in the form of a giant bird, a bat or bats that feast on blood" added Fr. K.

"Oh, hell! C'mon, Paul! My little girl was attacked by a flying, blood drinking demon? You've lost your minds!"

"Like I said, Mr. Helms you are free to believe what you want!" stated Msgr. C. as he again looked at Asa's clenched fist. Asa opened his hand and looked at the small pellets and back at the clergymen. After several seconds he realized that no matter what, his daughter was in danger.

Later that night a town meeting had been called in the church. Jakob Mueller presided. The town was essentially leaderless now and votes were held to elect the most eligible candidates. There was no mayor, no magistrate and no doctor. Until proper elections could be held it was decided that Jakob Mueller would serve as temporary mayor and Asa Helms and Harley McGuire would serve as temporary full time sheriff and deputy.

The meeting adjourned at ten o'clock p.m.

Asa had stayed up late reading some of the materials Fr. K. had lent to him. He thought that there had to be a more logical explanation, of course but much of what was happening could not be explained.

These deaths were happening to innocent people in a tiny town. There was no question that the destructive nature of the entities written about in these books definitely seemed to match some of the goings on here.

"My God, help us all" he said to himself. He knelt and prayed. Eva was awake, watching him. She rose out of her bed and knelt beside him. They were not Catholic or any denomination in particular but Asa held the rosary that Fr. K. had given him years ago as they recited the few prayers they knew together.

When they were done he kissed his daughter on the forehead and tucked her in. He looked into her eyes for a long while.

"What is it, dad?"

"Is Josh good to you?"

"What do you mean?" she replied looking away nervously.

"C'mon honey. I'm old but I ain't stupid".

She grew a look of concern on her face and said "Yes".

"I wish you'd stick with your own kind. He's a white man, honey". She frowned and looked away from him. "People talk, you know. People can get real mean. Lots, lots worse than you even know. Lots of stuff you don't expect can come up and cause a lot of woe between even jus' the two of you. What exactly is it you see in him?"

"Well, he's real handsome" she said smiling. "I don't know. He really liked me and said I was real pretty, prettier than any other girl he ever seen. He kept sayin' he was sorry for how he acted all that time and he just wanted to talk to me. So, we talked and then we talked some more. No man has ever liked me like this, dad. He takes me out with his friends and their girls. We have a real good time".

"Anything ever happens you tell me. He may have saved my life, but it'll be a good while before I feel right about this, if ever".

She nodded. "Okay, I will".

He kissed her again and blew out the candle.

Before midnight, Father Dennis prepared the letter Msgr. Clemente had written to the Vatican that afternoon. It was scheduled for delivery the next day. He was alone in the church. Several candles flickered and the light emitted strange shapes which danced around the walls and ceiling of the tent. Their motions made him uneasy, yet he wasn't ready for bed. He walked over to the cabinet in the corner and retrieved a bottle of whiskey and a glass. At the table he poured himself a drink, drank it immediately then poured another.

The wind picked up outside and he listened to the normally soothing sound of the whispering pines. The sound was hardly soothing this night, however. He finished his second drink and the lights moving around the room seemed to become more efficacious, almost violent. He was beginning to feel more on edge and poured a third drink and put the bottle away.

He drank the last whiskey and sat down to write in his journal. He wrote what he and his two cohorts had discussed in detail. In all they'd researched they agreed that the town was under siege by demonic ubiety. Karau was the first and prime suspect. He was first documented in Central and South America and most notably is referred to as the demon of devastation. He's known for brutally raping and mutilating his victims while causing destruction on many levels. These mutilations were beyond anything Fr. Dennis could even fathom. He thought of Father Stigg's hideous jack o'lantern head and crossed himself.

The attack on Eva also strongly matched aspects of demonic presence—the shape shifting tornado of bats and the lack of blood at the crime scenes weightily fit the description of Jilaiya, a demon best known in Asian-Indian culture. Two bats were extracted from her hair after the attack and examined. They were what are known as vampire bats, *not* native to North America. They survive by drinking blood. Rarely do they bite humans. Eva miraculously, was not bitten. Her father however, had suffered a small puncture wound under his arm which he did not even notice right away.

Fr. Dennis continued writing for some time and began to feel sleepy. He was tired, but he wanted to get as much as he could recorded before retiring. Nonetheless, his eyes began to close and his head nodded. Before long, he was fast asleep at his table.

When Fr. Dennis awoke he felt like he'd been asleep for hours. He looked at his watch and it had only been about forty minutes. He stood up amidst the still dancing lights from the candles. It was dark on the far side of the tent and he did not immediately see the figure standing in the corner. When he did notice, he glanced back and jumped in surprise with a shout.

"Whoa, Father! Scared the b'jeezus out of me! I was just getting ready for bed. Everything okay?"

There was no response. Fr. Dennis walked over to his cot and started to change into his bed clothes.

"Father?" he asked again. Once more, no reply.

He tilted his head and noticed that the figure standing in the tent wasn't nearly tall enough to be Fr. K. He picked up a candle and warily approached the intruder who was facing him. As he drew closer, he noticed that the man stood abnormally. He seemed disfigured, not hunchbacked, but may have suffered from leg or hip problems. He looked down at the man's feet and saw what appeared to be stumps. The man's legs shifted to the side and he grunted.

"Are you alright, sir? Do you need help?" asked Fr. Dennis. "Are you hungry or hur—".

He immediately stopped speaking when the light from the candle illuminated the man's face. The monk's expression was twisted in a terrible grimace of complete madness. His hair was wild and curly. He was covered in sweat, his fat, pale, unshaven face dripping with it. Father Dennis gasped in shock and breathing heavily, backed away.

The intruder came toward him with a strange, almost exaggerated limp. His mouth twisted in horrible fashion as his bulging eyes dilated. Fr. Dennis looked again to the man's feet. They were pointing *away* from him! With every step the man's robe collapsed inward where his knees should have been. *His legs were on backwards.*

TUESDAY, NOVEMBER 2, 1882.

Early that morning Asa walked from his cabin toward town. His head was throbbing. He was certain he'd run a fever overnight. The day before, he felt like he may be catching something—achy, a headache and a little bit of a sore throat. He sat at a table by the door at Amy's place. "Mornin' Asa. Coffee?" she asked.

"Yes, please. Thank you".

"Say, you alright? You look whiter than most folks around here".

He laughed and said "Feeling a little bit run down's all. Bound to happen at some point".

"True. I'll fetch some water too. Be right back".

Amy returned with his coffee, a glass of water and a cold wet rag. He wiped his face and brow. "Oh, that feels good, thank you". He breathed deeply and sat back in his chair and sipped some water.

"You hungry?" she asked.

"Not much, but s'pose I ought to eat somethin'". He took his first sip of coffee and gagged.

"Asa, you don't look very good at all". She put her hand on his forehead. He was burning up. "You should go home, you're on fire".

"Maybe so. I'd go see Dr. Stigg but I'm afraid he ain't gonna be much help". He replied smiling. She laughed and slapped him on the shoulder.

"Take the coffee with you. It might help some, if you can keep it down".

He stood up, wiped his face again with the cool rag and scratched under his arm where the bat had bitten him. It was getting itchier all the time. He walked to his cabin and laid down.

"Help! Somebody help! Please!" hollered Father Kettling as he ran into town.

"What is it?" Harley yelled from across the street.

"Father Dennis! He needs help! Hurry!"

Some men ran to the church. When they entered they found Father Dennis lying on his side on the dirt floor. He was badly hurt. His clothes were shredded around him as if he'd been attacked by a wild animal. A note was nailed to his right cheekbone. He was conscious. He was shaking in fear as he looked up at everyone who came to help. He was obviously in shock. He'd been violently slashed and beaten. "I'll get Asa!" said Kevin Marcks as he ran out of the tent.

Harley knelt down and gently took the note from the nail. "Father, can you hear me?" He nodded slowly in acknowledgement and opened his eyes. Fr. Dennis tried to speak. "Wha, w—w—wou—"

"Easy, Father" Fr. K said. "Catch your breath, son. You're going to be fine".

"He, he—" stammered Fr. Dennis swallowing hard and touching the nail in his face lightly and wincing in pain.

Msgr. Clemente briskly entered the tent. "What happened here, Paul?"

"I have no idea, Monsignor. I came in this morning and found him like this". The Monsignor knelt next to Fr. Dennis and spoke softly. "Denny, can you talk?"

Fr. Dennis took a couple of deep breaths and said " He.... ca—he came... for me. A warning. My leg is broken and my b-back, I thi—. Came to warn us".

"He? The monk?" Harley asked.

The injured man closed his eyes and nodded slowly.

"Could you see his face?"

"Yeth" he slurred. He was bleeding from his ear, nose and mouth. Hundreds of tiny cross shaped cuts and gashes covered his nearly naked body. Father Kettling grabbed the whiskey out of the cabinet and began clean the wound where the nail had been hammered. He turned and looked at Harley who was holding the bloodied note. Harley handed it to the Monsignor. "I ain't gonna read it" he said.

Msgr. Clemente read the note aloud. It read:

> Death's meter,
> Time will creep,
> This promise given,
> The Fallen will keep.
> Angel's Blade will fall....

"Is that the warning?" asked Asa as he entered the tent. He looked extremely ill. "Don't mind me folks, just a touch of the crud, I think. Kevin filled me in".

"Yesh. That's his warni'g" said Fr. Dennis propping himself on his left elbow, holding a cloth to his cheek. Wearily and in pain, he spoke. "He dows that a teeb from the Vatican is on its way and he will kill theb... all of us. He feeds on death and obscenity. I was....violated by him. There's no reason. He's just a glutton. They've done it all, eberythi'g and it's only goi'g to get worse".

"They?" asked Harley.

"Yeth, Karau and Jilaiya. They're real".

Fr. Dennis was cleaned up, bandaged and attended to in the church. The nail had carefully been removed from his cheek. He was speaking with Msgr. Clemente, Asa, Harley and Fr. Kettling. He was completely alert but visibly shaken to the core. His left shin had been broken but he was able to move his legs proving that his back suffered no paralyzing fracture.

"But, I haven't sent word to Rome with a formal request yet" Msgr. Clemente said. "Karau definitely said Vatican officials were on the way?".

"Yes, that's what he told me. I've never experienced such terrible, angry power. I didn't know it could be. I was going to send your letter today like you requested" Fr. Dennis replied.

"It's gotta be a trick" Asa said.

"I don't think so" said Fr. Dennis shaking his head. The fear in his eyes and his voice were obvious. "He's furious and said that we haven't even begun to imagine the horrors to come, so far it's been child's play. We haven't seen anything yet, so to speak".

The Monsignor stood and addressed the men. "Gentlemen, I think we are about to witness a battle of biblical proportions here. Right here in this little town".

WEDNESDAY, NOVEMBER 3, 1882.

Temporary mayor, Jakob Mueller and the three clergymen addressed the entire town outside of the church. Everyone was aware of the attack on Fr. Dennis. Most people of course refused to believe that actual demons were attacking them and their warnings were greeted with obscenities and laughter. Many cracked jokes and booed. Some even threw small rocks and food.

"Please! Please hear me!" shouted Jakob over the crowd. "Please, silence!" The jeering and the shouts became louder. The report of the gun behind him made him jump. Fr. Kettling stood with a smoking shotgun pointed toward the sky then stepped forward to the podium. The crowd stood silently and watched, stunned. "Shut the hell up!" he shouted as loudly as he could. His face was red and the veins in his temples pulsed. "I don't give a God damn if you believe this or not! Wanna stay here? Then stay! I don't care! But, mark my words, hell is here and it ain't turnin' back! I've lost m' best friends in this thing and I'm mad as hell! We all have! Friends *and* family! Think this is somethin' to laugh at, go ahead but do it on your own damned time! I swear to you right now the next sonofabitch that utters one sound is gonna get a gut full of shot! I mean it!"

The crowd stood, speechless at their pastor's outburst. Moments later, a man in the crowd started to say something and the irate priest stormed from the podium, walked into the crowd and shoved the barrels of his shotgun right in the man's face. "Can you hear me out here?" he yelled angrily. The man held his hands up and nodded. Jakob Mueller continued.

The entire town was warned right then and there. The clergymen did the best they could to explain how much danger everyone was in, but many of the town's population of three hundred refused to accept it. Others took heed to the warning and started discussing plans of evacuation. Others met to try and arrange some sort of defense. Most agreed that the church was the obvious point of protection and the large tent was moved close inside of town. No one was to go anywhere alone and watchmen were placed on duty round the clock.

THURSDAY, NOVEMBER 4, 1882.

A team of investigators from Rome arrived by coach late that morning. They had departed over two weeks ago after a letter was sent to Fr. Kettling denying a request for an investigation. The Pontiff had re-examined the happenings in the town after having repeatedly dreamt about them. He found the case extraordinary and was certain that God had guided him. He felt he should have acted sooner and dispatched a team without further delay.

The investigators were Vatican attorney, Fr. Kyle Richardson, Sister Marlena Carmen, Monsignor August O'Rourke and Fr. Alessio Fabiano. They were met by Fr. Kettling and Msgr. Clemente.

The team was shown their lodgings in a guest house in town owned by Jakob Mueller. After they settled in they visited Fr. Dennis who told them his story. Mass was said and the seven clergymen and woman went to Peckman's restaurant for a late lunch. Fr. Dennis walked the short distance slowly with a cane.

Over the meal they poured over their research. They all read separately, the warning so brutally delivered to Fr. Dennis:

> Death's meter,
> Time will creep,
> This promise given,
> The Fallen will keep.
> Angel's Blade will fall....

Msgr. O'Rourke was the expert in the field of demonology and explained in his thick, Irish accent what he thought the warning meant. "'Death's meter, time will creep' probably means that no matter how long it takes, he'll accomplish what he's set out to do. The Fallen is Karau and Jilaiya themselves, I believe.... if that's who... or what they really are."

"He told me that we are correct in referring to him as 'Karau' but he is also known by many other names. He mentioned some of them but I don't remember", said Fr. Dennis. "It's definitely him".

"Right, then, we'll not call him by his unholy name. Doing so may give him strength." O'Rourke continued. "Angel's Blade is us. There's no question of that. Maybe even the Pontiff himself. You said he was human. Can you describe him, Father?"

"Well, at first I thought he was Fr. K here but he was too short. I'm 5'11" or so and this man was maybe 5'4" or 5'5". He was fat and sweated horribly. He...., um... what he...what he—". His lip quivered and his eyes moistened as if he would cry.

"It's okay, Denny. Just describe what he looked like. That's all you have to do" said Msgr. Clemente calmly. Fr. Dennis nodded, composed himself and continued.

"He was wearing a Friar's robe and had wild curly hair, scraggly beard. I can't even describe the ugliness of the face. I've never seen anything like it- completely maniacal and.... *hideously* ugly. He has huge teeth. They're almost too big for his disgusting, fat head. Gahh... and his breath, like death! The most disturbing thing, however is that his legs are terribly deformed, almost as if they face... *backwards*, like the hind legs of a horse. He moved with unbelievable speed. Within moments I was completely helpless". He hung his head ashamed.

"You have nothing to be ashamed of Father" said Sr. Carmen.

"Of course not" O'Rourke proclaimed. "You're a strong man, sir and the Lord protected you".

Suddenly the wind whipped up violently, sending a cloud of dry dust high into the air. The door of the restaurant blew open and knocked over a chair. A man sitting nearby stood and closed it. As fast as it picked up, the wind died down and through the windows everyone could see him standing across the street- the monk stood, facing the restaurant.

Asa Helms tossed and turned in his bed. He was extremely ill. He was shivering, sweating profusely and was beginning to hallucinate. Eva did her best to make him comfortable. A doctor from Boulder had been summoned and was expected within a day or two.

In Asa's delirium, the tiny, one room cabin began to swell like a balloon. Every sound from the movement of his sheets to Eva's steps became exaggerated. He could feel his heartbeat pounding in his ears. He tried to relax but his breath became more and more labored.

The first bat flew in out of nowhere. Wide eyed, Asa watched it fly around the tiny room, crash into a window and fall to the floor, only to take flight again. A second appeared and flew directly at him. He waved it away and it missed his face with only its tiny wing slapping and stinging his cheek. Soon there was a third, then a fourth. Moments passed and more than a dozen now flew haphazardly around the room, slamming into the walls, pots and pans, the windows *and Eva.* She strangely continued her work unaffected. He yelled for her to take cover but she looked at him in total confusion.

"What's wrong, pa? You're okay. Need s'more water?"

He couldn't figure out why she was behaving so calmly with these horrible, little creatures flying around their cabin.

Suddenly and all at once they attacked Asa. Tiny teeth and claws inflicted awful wounds to his face and body.

He screamed at Eva to get out! She was now barely visible through the cloud of bats. He reached for her, swatting at the vermin around her. Eva tried to restrain him as he pulled her down to him and rolled on top of her. She took this to mean only one thing and fiercely resisted. She didn't understand what in the world he was seeing or thinking.

She screamed at him to get off and punched him in the face as hard as she could again and again. She was very small under his six foot, 190 pound frame. He wasn't molesting her but she was pinned. She finally realized that he was trying to protect her from something she couldn't see. She yelled at the top of her lungs, "Daddy, it's gone! It's gone! Gone! It's gone, daddy!"

He looked over his shoulder and saw an empty room. "What the —? Where'd they go?" His rapid breathing continued and his eyes frantically darted around the room for any sign of the invaders.

"It ain't there no more, just disappeared, daddy. It's okay now, you can get offa me. You're smushin' me." He rolled off, cautiously let her up and vomited in the bucket next to his bed. He rolled his eyes and was looking at her when he fainted.

She cleaned him up and soaked a fresh sheet in cold water and covered him. He was burning up with fever.

"It's him! That's him!" said a visibly agitated Fr. Dennis from inside the restaurant. The monk's hood was pulled over his head. This time he held a long staff at his side. People stopped in the street and stared. Everyone was shocked by his boldness and weren't sure how to react at first. He seemed to just appear out of nowhere. Some drew their guns. Others sought to get far away from what they knew would be a fight.

The clergy, completely amazed at his suddenness in making an appearance wasted no time themselves. They immediately walked from the restaurant to confront him. Kevin, Harley, Fr. Kettling and three other men pointed their guns and surrounded the killer, remaining careful to keep a safe distance.

Fr. O'Rourke immediately addressed the monk. "We know who you are. You are filthy, unholy and inhuman. We will defeat you. Set yourself afire and cleanse this place of your vileness". The entity did not respond.

Sister Carmen quickly pulled out a small vial of holy water and threw it on the monk. He stepped backwards and in a flash, jammed the end of the staff into her face, hard! "Whore!" he shouted in a disgusting guttural voice and laughed. Blood gushed from her nose as she cried out.

"Back to Hell with you!" O'Rourke shouted as he threw his own holy water. The monk's laugh ceased. He seized the Monsignor by the throat and sprinted toward the restaurant at shocking speed, his bizarre, deformed gait carrying him. He slammed the man's head into a support beam and O'Rourke fell to his knees, landing face down in the dirt, unconscious. Fr. Dennis limped out of the restaurant and crouched at his side to try and help.

Fr. Kettling ran at the monk and fired both barrels of his shotgun, point blank into his back. The robe exploded with dust. *Its* body jerked sideways and it stumbled but never went down.

Moments passed, everyone watched. It was apparent the hideous assailant had, in fact been seriously injured by the shotgun blast. It grunted and gasped as it attempted to reach around its fat, bloated body to find the wound.

Father Kettling gritted his teeth and started to reload when the the monk turned and met his shooter's eyes with a fury.

The priest froze in terror but like hell if he was going to let the bastard see his fear.

As they locked eyes, the priest's own fury mounted as he stared into the seemingly empty hood. He knew he was making eye contact and raised his gun, preparing to blast the monster's head off when suddenly, *it barked.* Mucous and blood spewed from its mouth, spraying Fr. K. who incredibly seemed unaffected by the disgusting shower.

The monk backed away and its head moved quickly and repeatedly, watching those around it with caution as it clumsily circled in place, eyeing its attackers. Clearly frightened, it stopped moving, raised its arms and unleashed an un-Godly scream of angry terror.

At that, thousands of crows began squawking loudly from every direction of the surrounding forest. They grew louder and louder and angrier and angrier as the seconds passed.

With one more shriek, the monk turned and ran clumsily, straight for the woods.

Everyone was too stunned to chase him, but the moment they saw him enter the tree line, an enormous army of crows rose from the forest and circled above like a giant, black hurricane. They screeched in unison, an ear-piercing chorus making it clear that they were an army hell bent on destruction.

Harley recognized the threat and wasted no time. He yelled as loudly as he could for everyone to take cover as he lifted Sr. Carmen under his arm and sprinted back toward the restaurant as the murder of crows began their attack.

Everyone scattered. People dove under wagons and carriages, ran into buildings or crouched behind posts and troughs. Many did not make it to safety.

The birds careened violently into buildings, knocking out windows, seriously injuring horses and people in the process.

They flew at the newly relocated church tent, knocking it down, shredding it.

The attack lasted not even a minute. After their destructive rampage, the surviving crows spiraled like a tornado, straight up and veered north toward the Helms' property.

Eva could see the giant mass of birds attack the town from her yard. She heard the glass from windows shatter as the impacts of hundreds of feathered bodies slammed into wood and stone. The terrible sounds echoed through the valley.

Now they were heading in her direction. The birds flew low, up the valley and came right at her but did not attack. At the last second they shot straight up ninety degrees and dispersed, soaring high and away. Their squawks faded into the distance and everything slowly became quiet.

In the silence that followed, stunned, she began to hear the rising cries and screams from town. She wondered if she should leave her ill father and try to help, but her thoughts were cut short by a growing choir of growling coyotes in the tree line, merely yards from where she stood. A slight breeze blew her hair into her face and she started to back slowly toward the cabin.

Her eyes darted back and forth searching for any signs of the threat as the growls became louder, more guttural.

Her breath increased and she turned to run when an entire band of coyotes charged from the trees!

The first grabbed her ankle. Its hold was terribly strong. She screamed, struggling to get away as a second animal latched onto her left forearm. "Help me!" she shrieked. "Help me!" A third bit into her right side, tearing her flesh. Two others struggled to pull her to the ground.

She almost went down when her father burst from the cabin door with his Winchester.

With steady aim, Asa fired, hitting the first in the head, dropping it immediately. He fired at another which also fell.

The animals tore at Eva's legs and side as another lunged at her throat. She turned, barely deflecting the strike.

Several wasted no time in turning their attack on Asa. They charged and easily pulled him to the ground. He was weak from fever but he managed to roll onto his stomach, aim and shoot. He fired again and again in spite of the vicious attackers tearing into his back, neck and legs.

Finally, he could no longer control the weapon. He rolled onto his back, swung and jabbed the butt of his rifle at the coyotes, clumsily clubbing them off. One clamped onto his right hand. With his left, he managed to steady the gun under his chin, aim and fire. That one last miraculous shot freed Eva who ran inside the cabin and slammed the door behind her.

She watched out the window helplessly as her father became overwhelmed by the animals. She picked up Ely's Peacemaker, broke the glass and fired. With the gun in both hands and six shots in the chamber, four bullets found their mark. Wounded, one coyote ran back into the trees. Another was hit in the spine and collapsed, yelping loudly. The other two dropped with wounds to the torsos.

Josh and a group of men from town rode up on horseback and immediately began shooting the beasts. They fell, one after the other. One made an attempt to latch onto one of the horse's hind legs which replied by kicking the animal so hard, it flew ten feet into the air and landed with a thud. The animal yelped upon impact and limped on three legs back into the tree line.

Realizing they were outnumbered, the surviving mongrels fled into the trees and again, silence fell on the settlement.

The sun was setting and Asa lay motionless in the tall grass. He'd been viciously attacked and had quickly bled out from bites to his throat and legs. He was dead. Josh stood up from the body and walked to the cabin and up the steps where Eva stood in shock. He held her arms, looked into her eyes and shook his head. She tried to run past him to get to her father but Josh held her tightly.

"Daddy! Help him! Help him! Daddy!" she shrieked in panic and horror. Josh struggled to hold her. Finally, she fell to her knees, sobbing hysterically. He held her tightly, now crying himself. The other men wrapped her father's body in a blanket and delivered him to town.

FRIDAY, NOVEMBER 5, 1882.

Asa Helms had been the town sheriff, a black man hastily and not without conflict elected on a temporary basis. He had been a leader and a fighter. The town mourned his passing and without him and Ely they lacked strong leadership. His funeral was quickly arranged that morning and Fr. Kettling said Mass. Asa was buried in a plot on his property with a simple cross and his badge marking the spot as Eva had requested.

To most, especially those with children and families, enough was enough and many began packing up to leave for good. Approximately half the remaining population of Tahosa would now abandon the town.

Msgr. O'Rourke had suffered a small skull fracture from the attack. He had been recovering inside the restaurant and could not see clearly out of his left eye. He'd regained consciousness the night before and was alert.

Sister Carmen's nose had been broken.

Stewart and Kevin Marcks along with Harley McGuire joined Amy and the clergy personnel in the restaurant that afternoon.

"It has begun—a true war between God and Satan" O'Rourke said groggily. "We might have the upper hand. We have an idea of what can hurt it and from all we've studied we may be able to kill it".

"If only we had the angels to help us" Fr. Kyle said in his usual annoyingly dramatic fashion.

"We do have the angels" replied Fr. Kettling. "These men and women who fought and died are some of the most powerful here."

"How do you kill something like that?" asked Amy.

"Holy Fire" O'Rourke said. "The only problem is that Holy Fire happens in only one place, Jesus' tomb in the Church of the Holy Sepulchre in Jerusalem".

"It also happens only on Holy Saturday of every year, Easter's Eve, if you will" added Fr. Dennis.

"How the hell do we arrange that? We can't wait that long. It'd be way past Easter by the time they got a flame to us, if that's even possible" Stewart added gruffly.

"Holy Fire exists in the Orthodox Church, not the Catholic. However, many on both sides have experienced its miracle" said Sr. Carmen. Both of her eyes were black and she sounded terribly nasally. "I think it's worth a try".

"We're supposed to hang around here and be picked off until weeks after Easter?" Fr. Kettling said. "Not me, I've had enough".

"Father, you can't leave!" said Amy. "You're our pastor for God's sake!"

"Oh, Amy I know it. I'm not goin' anywhere. Just sayin' that we need to figure something out here, that's all".

Several stocked wagons, horses and two buggies stopped in front of the restaurant. Jakob and Erick Mueller entered the room.

Jakob stood in silence and made eye contact with everyone. The overwhelming sadness in his eyes was heartbreaking. He cleared his throat and spoke in a strong, yet shaky voice.

"Ladies und gentlemen, Most of my employees are gone. I can't afford to keep der mine open. My son has been killed and my family and I vill relocate. Ve are leaving for Denver immediately".

His voice wavered and cracked as he spoke. "Please, please know that all of you have fought valiantly und bravely. My family und I vish you der best of luck und God's graces. God bless you all and zank you zo, zo much from der bottom of my heart. May God be vis you all".

It was that short and simple. In an afternoon, the Mueller family made the decision and packed what they had left. Goodbyes were said and hugs were exchanged. Eva, who was recovering at the trading post came with Josh to say her good-byes to the family. She and Josh had decided to also leave. In less than twenty four hours they would ride south toward Boulder.

The exodus out of town was growing.

PART 10

THIRTY EIGHT

THURSDAY, NOVEMBER 11, 1882.

THE MINE WAS completely abandoned. Its entrance was boarded over and Jakob Mueller had made arrangements to sell it immediately upon his return to Denver.

Less than seventy people now occupied the town of Tahosa. Fathers Kettling, Dennis, Fr's. Kyle Richardson and Alessio Fabiano along with Msgrs. O'Rourke, Clemente and Sister Carmen prepared for what they hoped would be a final offensive against the demons that had destroyed the town.

The purple lights from the area of the mine were visible over the last two nights by Harley and Kevin, the only remaining law enforcement team. The men patrolled the settlement, the cemetery and up to the mine and back every night. Upon seeing the lights, they returned immediately to town. No chances were to be taken.

After their rounds this night, the men went immediately to the saloon. A band of fourteen Lakota Indians entered soon after.

"Can I help you men?" asked Stewart. A short man who appeared to be their leader spoke.

"We came to try to help. We have heard the stories of Iya".

"Iya?", asked Stew.

"The great evil spirit. Your 'devil'. We have seen the lights on the mountain".

"Where're you fellas from?"

"North. Lakota lands"

"Ain't you a bit far from home? You don't want to be here, trust me".

"On the other hand, we need all the help we can get" said Harley. "What have you heard?"

"We arrived four nights ago" the Lakota leader replied. "We are camped to the east".

Over whiskey and beer, the Lakota men told what they'd heard and how far word had spread.

They advised that they were already preparing their own offensive against the evil invaders. Lakota spiritualism and power was about to be unleashed stronger than it ever had been in these people's history.

FRIDAY, NOVEMBER 12, 1882, 6:00 AM

After sunup, deep in the mine where Dr. Stigg had been found, the demon disguised as a Catholic monk, Karau sat, slumped and covered in sweat. The shotgun blasts from the bastard priest had done more damage than it first thought. It wasn't able to reach the deep, ghastly holes in its back to remove the shot. Its spine had been so damaged, it severely limited movement. The demon was now in danger... and it knew it.

It heard the beating of drums above ground and the boards being torn away from the mine entrance. The weak, pathetic Indians were starting their filthy rituals or whatever they were doing. Somehow, they knew he was there. As badly injured as it had been there would be no way for a quick, easy escape. The damned Indians weren't going to leave until after the tiny group of clergy excrement joined them. Even though the demon's motion was limited, between its powers and its cohort, Jilaiya the small force of humans would be wiped out. The thought was pleasing.

It stood with great difficulty and fell sideways against the tunnel wall. *Pain* it thought. Something it wasn't used to racked its bloated, sweaty, pale, hair matted body. Its tongue hung out of its mouth and the demon fell again, its chin thudding against the hard rock floor. The jolt caused the gigantic, yellowed teeth to slam shut, severing its lower lip. The bloody lip hung from the mouth like a leech and several bats flew onto its disgusting face and hungrily lapped up the blood. Irritated, Karau swatted them away.

The drums continued and it groaned with irritation. It was beginning to smell the smoke from the sage fires the Lakota band had started. Sage, according to Lakota faith would hopefully calm the demons.

All clergy personnel along with Harley and Kevin rode up to the Mueller mine. They travelled in a wagon which had been filled with buckets and vessels of holy water which Msgr. Clemente had blessed that morning. Everyone was armed to the teeth, including tiny Sr. Carmen who brandished a .12 gauge, double barrel coach shotgun. They prayed the Rosary on the way.

The band of Lakotas had stayed up all evening drumming and praying loudly. The drums could be heard all the way into town.

As O'Rourke and the others approached, the Lakota holy man, Running Wolf was directing sage smoke into the entrance of the mine with a pine bough as he murmured his incantations. He waved a large eagle feather with his right hand in an attempt to absorb and trap the spirits.

Deep in the mine, Karau and Jilaiya had been made sluggish by the smoke and Running Wolf's words. They couldn't hear him, but they *felt* the effects of his practice. The constant sound of the drums had aggravated Karau so much he'd broken both hands punching the tunnel walls in rage.

Jiliaya, having possessed an entire colony of bats flew noisily with such intense speed through the tunnels and caverns, that hundreds were killed. Their tiny, furry bodies slammed violently into walls, ceilings and abandoned equipment.

Karau felt their presence immediately—The Christian filth had arrived. It could feel the prayers of dozens granting power and strategy to its nemesis. The Indians had kept it at bay but now it was time to fight.

Simultaneously, the clergy prayed aloud together as they prepared for the assault. The buckets of holy water were strategically placed.

Uninterrupted, Running Wolf continued what he was doing.

Prepared, the members of the clergy stood facing the mine in a half circle around Running Wolf. They had joined hands and were now loudly reciting the Lord's Prayer. The drums thundered, echoing through the mountains and valleys.

Moments passed when, without warning, thousands of bats exploded from the mine entrance with a deafening roar. Msgr. O'Rourke was ready in an instant and launched a bucket of holy water at the attacking mass. The shrieking bats parted where the shower of water struck and the voice of Jilaiya screamed collectively.

Around him, O'Rourke's companions were immediately and viciously attacked as tiny teeth and claws bit and scratched flesh. The others poured vessels of holy water over each other and shouted prayers. Several bats flew into the mouths of Fathers Kyle and Kettling, ravaging their tongues, cheeks and gums. The attack was violent and terrible.

Father Kettling dropped his bottle of holy water which shattered on the ground. Collapsing to his knees he shielded his eyes while attempting to pull the violators from his lips, ears, hands and hair. Msgr. Clemente poured a full bucket of the water over him and the rodents retreated, many refreshing their attacks on Indians.

Sr. Carmen was drenched in water. She had jumped into the wagon and was now throwing water on anyone who needed it. *A fire would be more tolerable* she thought. Blood poured from her eyebrows, cheeks, hands and ears where she'd been bitten but she did not stop.

Kevin and Harley did their best to help the Indians fan the heavy smoke with large, fur pine branches. The bats were not as thick where the fires burned. Nonetheless, Kevin's entire left hear and most of his right eye had already been chewed away. He and Harley, who was also horribly maimed worked bravely to fight the entities.

Four of the Indians refused to stop beating the drums as they were attacked. Their flesh was chewed and torn.

Running Wolf fell and rolled on the ground, shouting in horror and pain as hundreds of bats completely covered him. Sister Carmen did her best to drench him but he was too far away. She screamed for him to roll toward her but he couldn't hear over the commotion. The tiny woman grabbed two full buckets and, in one giant leap jumped from the back of the wagon to a spot near him. Her leg broke at the knee and the bloody bone ripped through the skin as if it was tissue paper. She cried out but held firm. The buckets did not spill. On one foot she stood and poured a full bucket over the holy man. The attacking bats shot from their prey and flew straight up, scattering in the trees. She doused him with another bucket and he groaned in pain.

Most of the defenders were now drenched. The water served as a relatively strong repellant. Most of it had been used and more was needed. Father Fabiano took the initiative and boarded the wagon and sped back to town. He would bless it himself. He prayed loudly the entire ride. Chewed up and bloodied from the attack, the horses pulling the rig galloped stealthily. For a brief moment the priest saw a rider pass him with astonishing speed and gallop ahead, quickly vanishing into thin air. Although brief, Fr. Fabiano could see the rider rode a white horse and wore a bright blue coat and a black hat over long, blond hair. He radiated almost blinding, golden light. *I think I'm being escorted* he thought. In no time he was in town.

Townsfolk knew what was needed and had already filled dozens of vessels with water. His wagon hadn't even stopped when everyone began loading it. Four men on horseback now charged up the trail toward the mine to join the fight.

As the wagon was being loaded Fr. Fabiano stood in his driver's seat and blessed the water. Within minutes, the wagon was full and he sat down and snapped the reigns. The horses turned and thundered back up the mountain undaunted.

As Fr. Fabiano returned to the mine, he could see the men who'd just left town ahead of him. They were under attack. Two of them were on the ground. One sprinted back down the trail passing him and another fell to the ground, beating at his assailants. Their horses had bolted. The other two men were still on horseback trying their best to keep from being bucked. One rider was thrown and he landed on his head, breaking his neck, killing him instantly. The other man dismounted in the fray and swatted his horse which ran back down the trail. He then fell to the ground and tried to defend himself. The priest prodded the horses forward and pulled up next to the man, immediately dousing him. The attackers retreated but it was merely seconds before another torrent of bats attacked the priest for a second time that day.

Even though he was being chewed alive, Fr. Fabiano calmly doused himself which caused most of the vermin to disperse into the trees above. Many still went for his face and ears. Shielding himself with his arm, he tried to reach behind and grab a second water vessel. He fumbled blindly and was about to jump from the driver's seat and flee when a heavy wall of water crashed into him from both sides. The rodents flew straight up and away.

Catching his breath and wiping his face with his hands, he looked down. A young Lakota brave stood to each side of him holding an empty bucket. They were smiling as they stared up at him. Tied in their hair and clothing were smoldering bundles of sage. The priest smiled back and almost laughed.

As Fr. Fabiano looked around, he saw that the bats had diminished significantly. They seemed to be scattering in confusion.

The survivors again doused themselves, each other and the wounded with fresh holy water. The huge fires were again stoked and fanned. This dissuaded further attacks and the bats retreated for good.

Finally, releasing its tiny hosts, the invisible and defeated Jiliaya withdrew back into its own lonely hell.

Msgr. O'Rourke lay face up in the dirt, wet and bluish in color. Fathers Fabiano and Kyle knelt next to him. It appeared that his heart had given out. "It was fast", said Sr. Carmen who laid mere feet away with her crucifix and rosary in hand. "He was trying to help me when he just fell. I think he was gone before he hit the ground". Two Lakota men were cleaning her wounds and preparing to move her back to town.

Several Indians lay near the entrance of the mine, their faces mutilated beyond recognition. Strangely, their fingers, knees and elbows were completely gone. Kevin Marcks had been assisting the Indians with keeping the fires and smoke going when he was attacked repeatedly and ruthlessly. Hundreds of bats had torn into his upper legs and throat, severing the major arteries. He had fought hard before rapidly bleeding out. His corpse now sat slumped against a tree. Harley crouched next to him, stunned.

Harley was bleeding profusely from his own wounds. The bats had done horrible damage—he had no right eye and both ears had been completely chewed away. His other eye was mostly swollen shut. Blood poured from his throat in a thick, steady stream. He knew it was perhaps moments before he bled to death. He became extremely dizzy and faint when he heard the approaching gallop of a horse and what he thought was Stewart Marcks' loud, trembling voice.

"No! No! No! No! Oh, my boy! My boy!" Cried Stewart as he jumped from his horse and knelt down to hold his dead son. "Oh, sweet Jesus, help me….help me! No….no….oh no!" He bowed his head and sobbed loudly.

Harley was reaching out to him when dizziness overwhelmed him and he tipped forward into the blood drenched dirt. As he drifted away he heard a piano and stood to follow it. The sound was coming from somewhere up the mountain. The dizziness was gone and toward the end of a huge, remarkably bright light which appeared before him he could see the distant figure of his mother playing her old, out of tune, upright piano. She'd taught him to play until she died when he was just thirteen. She stood and smiled at him with a warm, radiant and beautiful smile. He ran to her and they embraced in a joyous reunion. Harley looked back and saw his smiling friend, Kevin running to them.

The three went into the light together.

Fr. Kettling was pulling himself back toward the mine. He was laying yards away in the woods. He wasn't able to stand

and tried pulling himself up by his elbows. Running Wolf, who had known the priest vaguely for decades saw him and ran to help. Both men were covered in blood.

"Father, can you stand?" asked the Indian.

"You speak English? All these years I didn't know you could speak English" said the priest.

"Of course I speak English. I just never liked you very much. I didn't want to talk to you, until now anyway. You fight like a very angry woman".

"What? A woman?"

"It's a good thing. You fight fiercely"

"Hmph" grunted Fr. K. as Running Wolf helped him to his feet.

When they returned to the mine entrance, the men were aghast at the destruction around them. Injured, dead or dying laid among the hundreds of bat corpses. They knelt beside O'Rourke's body and Fr. K. crossed himself. He looked at the bone protruding from Sr. Carmen's leg.

"Oh, Sr. Carmen, I'm so sorry. Is there anything I can do?" he said.

"It's so painful. These young men tried to push it back but it's no use" she said. "I passed out and they kept trying. I will probably lose it but it won't kill me".

Father Kyle spoke. "Sister, God bless you. You will survive and know that you have fought as valiantly as any man here. You are a hero and will one day be heavily rewarded". Annoyed and somewhat insulted at what she considered a rather sexist comment, she looked up at him and started laughing. She said "Bullshit, Kyle. You're such a goody-goody sugar flows out of your ass. Stop it for once, would you? You're making me sick". They all laughed.

Karau was almost to the entrance of the mine as the demon slowly and clumsily walked, leaning heavily on its staff. Its supernatural power had been enough to sustain its human host this long, but it had been weakened significantly by the combination of bullet wounds; and now massive assaults of sage and prayer. It no longer had the power to leave this body and possess another. Not one of its awaiting enemies were spiritually weak enough to inhabit. *Time was running out.*

Its unintelligible grumble became audible shouts of hatred and anger as it entered the daylight. The crowd of Indians and clergy were waiting for him.

Father Kettling and Running Wolf approached the demon. Father K spoke:

"We beat one of you, now we're going to send you back to hell to join your friend. Ready, filth?"

Karau stared hoodless at the faces looking back at it. Its eyes were wide and its face and robes were soaked in sweat. "Gra.... graway!" it shouted as blood and spit flew from its deformed mouth. You fight like children! You have no idea of the power I have!" Father Dennis cringed at the sound of the familiar, guttural wet voice. "I have—"

His speech stopped abruptly as a Lakota warrior behind swung his tomahawk full force. The stone plunged deeply into the back of the demon's skull. Gore splattered everywhere. The brave withdrew the weapon and swung again, this time hitting the top of its spine with a loud *crack*. Karau immediately fell backwards and landed with a disgusting thud in the dirt. Everyone crowded around it and peered down. Karau stared back up at them in surprise.

It knew what it wanted to say and tried to speak, "Heegh… wol…. all….!" The tongue hung out of its mouth, jostling the severed lip. Karau was shaking and began to try to stand.

Running Wolf stepped forward with his eagle feather in his right hand and resumed incantations. Behind, the drums again began to thunder loudly. The clergy held their crucifixes and together again recited the Lord's prayer.

The massive assault of prayer agitated Karau so much it made one last effort to fight. Grabbing Running Wolf's ankle, it pulled as hard as it could. The small holy man's weight did not shift at all as he continued praying, staring down at the pathetic demon.

"I am Running Wolf. You are Iya, the most vile of spirits. It is time to go back where you came from. You no longer have power here".

With that, the drums became even louder and the surrounding Indians jammed flaming torches into the demon's repugnant flesh and clothing. As it ignited, it shrieked loudly and horribly. Suddenly, with a loud "whoosh", the feather in Running Wolf's hand burst into a large white flame. The holy man jumped backwards, flinching from the fire which engulfed his hand, yet it did not burn him.

Karau's human host body began to burn as fast as dry kindling, crackling and bubbling.

Running Wolf stared in amazement at the white flame dancing on his fist. Msgr. Clemente reached out and scooped a flame into his own hand and held it. He then passed flame to the others. Soon, all of the survivors, including the wounded held a bright white, dancing flame in his and her hands. No one was burned.

Father Fabiano crossed himself and knelt. "Holy Fire!" he stated as he started to cry. The clergy knelt around him as

Running Wolf held his flaming fist to the sky and whooped loudly in victory. The horrible battle had ended and the tiny army had fought and won.

Father Fabiano had seen him only briefly on the trail. The archangel, Michael stood next to his white horse atop the mountain looking down into the valley below. His long blond hair flew into his bearded face and he brushed it from his eyes. The remnants of Tahosa were visible in the distance.

His bright blue coat fluttered in the wind as he placed a clay container which had carried the Miracle of Holy Fire to Tahosa in his satchel.

Standing with him, the smiling spirit of a jolly, fattened, curly blond-headed Friar named John Nickelby waited to accompany him to heaven. He was free now.

Karau had simply taken advantage of a good and charitable man in his moment of doubt—a hearty and giving man who travelled alone in his oversized, purple covered wagon during the holidays offering gifts and a magic show to the orphanages of the Rocky Mountains.

THIRTY NINE

July 5, 2014. Rocky Mountain National Park, Colorado.

BILL AND JANNIE ate their lunches on the banks of the river. "What's out here that's so important? You seemed like you were in such a hurry" He asked. "I thought we were just going to hike in a few miles. We've gone like…. at least ten. I'm wiped."

"I know. I'm sorry. I just wanted to see it, always have".

"See what?" he asked as he looked around.

"There used to be a town here" she replied cheerfully.

"Really? I see nothing whatsoever indicating mankind ever occupied this place".

"Smart ass. My grandparents and parents talked about this place my whole life" Jannie replied. "This was my great-great grandparents' town".

"No shit?' he asked.

"No shit. There's a mine up there in the hills somewhere. Maybe we can look for it tomorrow. In the 1800's a bunch of people were murdered and bunch more died in a fire. Then it was completely abandoned, I guess. My grandma said her great-grandpa was actually the sheriff. One of the few black sheriffs ever, back then, anyway."

Aside from a few rotted, overgrown foundations, the only other evidence that anyone had lived in what used to be the town of Tahosa, CO was a cemetery half a mile away that they would never see. Nor would they see the one lone grave in the valley where a rusted badge still lay where a hero was buried 132 years before.

Bill and Jannie pitched camp and made a fire. Bill opened the cooler, handed her a beer and cracked one open for himself. As the sun began to set, Jannie curled up with her man and told the story of her great-great grandparents, Josh and Eva Adams.

Far above the valley, hidden away in the trees rested the huge, dilapidated wagon. Its original deep purple color had faded long ago.

THE END

AFTERWORD

Lakota practice holds that sage smoke is used in attempt to calm evil spirits. An eagle feather is held by a holy man during rites in the belief that the entity will be absorbed and trapped.

In the Orthodox Church, the Church of the Holy Sepulchre in Jerusalem annually reveals the miracle of Holy Fire. Many Catholics also embrace this miracle.

Do demons exist? Well, that's up to you. I believe they do, but I have no idea what one looks or sounds like. I've never met one. Not that I know of, anyway, (unless you count my high school driver's ed instructor). Nonetheless, I'd say many may exist right here among us, great or small. You can ask if terrorist factions or Hitler, for that matter are demons. Are they? Maybe, maybe not....Who's to say what a demon is or isn't? Whatever the case, it has been documented that demons can, and have taken human form as did Karau throughout world history.

In this story, God worked jointly through Catholic, Orthodox and Lakota faiths to help Kill Karau and send Jiliaya back to Hell. Once Karau's spirit was absorbed into the eagle feather and trapped, the miracle of Holy Fire consumed and destroyed it. Would or does God work this way? Why not? I believe God works through all of us to defeat evil, no matter what the culture and history of a people. Besides, who's to say one faith is more powerful than another or that they don't work together?

HISTORY NOTE

If you're a Colorado history buff, you'd know that the Denver Archdiocese was not actually founded until 1887, but who cares? It's a story.

Another thing, a nun would not likely have travelled with the clergy of the time for such a mission, but again….it's a story.

If you're an American history buff, you'd know that there were in fact black sheriffs, marshals and deputies in the old west. Bass Reeves, who was Deputy U.S. Marshal for the Western District of Arkansas is definitely worth researching. He served for something like 30 years until he retired in 1893. He was no one to reckon with. Look him up, he's fascinating!

The US Government Wars against against the Lakota Sioux had ended, for the most part by the early 1880's. There were still problems, however, i.e. the massacre at Wounded Knee in 1890. Missions and Indian agencies did exist to help affected communities.

Very few, if any Lakota people lived South of Nebraska. (Stewart Marcks hints at this in the story). Their faith and fighting spirit fascinate me, however. Same could be said for *any* American Indian tribe, of course, but I picked the Lakota Sioux because I wanted to, that's all.

The characters of Karau and Jiliaya are told in the story as they are told in the cultural histories specified in "The Tahosa

Monk". Generally, Jiliaya would possess a bird, birds or bats, but for the entertainment value in this story, it also possessed a band of coyotes.

A lot of folks may argue with me over whether or not mixed relationships happened in the Old West. They did, of course. Here's three very famous examples: Kit Carson, Belle Starr and Charles Bowdre. All were in intermixed marriages.

There was never a Mueller Silver Mine, but there is a Tahosa Trading Post. I used to buy stuff there when I was a kid. It still stands near Boulder, CO.

Lastly, Tahosa is a real place and it's where I first had a notion for the idea for "The Tahosa Monk" when I was just 12 years old. It's stayed with me all this time and I hope you enjoyed it.

Thank you very much for taking the time to read the book.

God bless,
Michael Anthony May

Thank you....
Jerry and Barbara May
Daniel Paschke
Brian Rempel
Maryanne Davis
John Moore

and Vicki Wadleigh, the hardest working person I know.
In memory of Jolie.

ABOUT THE AUTHOR

*photo by Christopher Grommesh

Michael Anthony May is a writer, actor and musician based in
Denver, CO.
A Dr. Mayhem Productions and Sound Design creation.
Visit www.doctor-mayhem.com for more information.